Andreï Makine

A Life's Music

Translated by Geoffrey Strachan

SCEPTRE

Copyright © 2001 Andreï Makine
French edition © 2001 Éditions du Seuil
Translation © 2002 Geoffrey Strachan

First published in Great Britain in 2002 by Hodder and Stoughton
A division of Hodder Headline

A Sceptre Paperback

The right of Andreï Makine to be identified as the Author
of the Work has been asserted by him in accordance with the
Copyright, Designs and Patents Act 1988.

1

A CIP catalogue record for this title is
available from the British Library

ISBN 0 340 82009 8

Typeset in Sabon by Palimpsest Book Production Limited,
Polmont, Stirlingshire
Printed and bound in Great Britain by
Clays Ltd, St Ives plc

Hodder and Stoughton
A division of Hodder Headline
338 Euston Road
London NW1 3BH

Translator's note

Andreï Makine was born and brought up in Russia but *A Life's Music*, like his other novels, was written in French. The book is set in Russia and the author uses some Russian words in the French text which I have kept in this English translation. These include: *shapka* (a fur hat or cap, often with earflaps); *dacha* (a country house or cottage, typically used as a second or holiday home); *izba* (a traditional wooden house built of logs); and *taiga* (the virgin pine forest that spreads across Siberia south of the tundra).

The text contains references to several well-known Russian place names including the Nevsky Prospekt, the street in St Petersburg (on the river Neva); and in Moscow the Stone Bridge and Arbat, the famous street in the city centre; as well as to Graben, the street at the heart of Vienna.

I am indebted to a number of people, including the author, for advice, assistance and encouragement in the preparation of this translation. To all of them my thanks are due, notably Malcolm Borthwick, Ludmilla Checkley, June Elks, Don Hill, Pierre Sciama, Claire Squires, Simon Strachan, Susan Strachan and, above all, my editor at Sceptre, Carole Welch.

G.S.

I could quite easily put a date to that encounter. It goes back at least a quarter of a century. More precisely, to the year when a celebrated philosopher, then a refugee in Munich, coined a phrase that quickly gained currency, an expression thinkers, politicians and even mere mortals would go on using for a good decade or more throughout the world. The extraordinary success enjoyed by his formula stemmed from one palpable merit: in two Latin words the philosopher had succeeded in summing up the lives of all two hundred and forty million of the human beings who at that time peopled the land of my birth. Women and men, children and adults, old people and new-born babies, the dead and the living, the sick and the healthy, innocents and murderers, the learned and the ignorant, workers in the depths of coal mines, cosmonauts in their celestial orbits; these and thousands of other categories of people were all linked to a common essence by this innovative expression. They all began to exist under one generic name.

Both before and since this inspired invention, people have endlessly dreamed up combinations of words to characterize the country in question. 'The evil empire', 'barbarism with a human face', 'the shattered empire' . . . Each of these locutions made its mark on western minds for a time. But the Munich philosopher's definition was by far the most often used and the most enduring.

To such an extent that, barely a few months after the phrase made its appearance, I heard it on the lips of a friend who lived, like me, on the banks of the Neva, listened secretly, like so many others, to western radio stations and had heard an interview with the philosopher. To such an extent, indeed, that once, when I was returning from a trip to the Far East, and was held up by a snowstorm somewhere in the heart of the Urals, I recalled this term, extolled in the West but prohibited in our country, and spent part of the night applying it to the passengers who surrounded me in the waiting-room of a dark, icy railway station. The term invented by the philosopher proved to be devastatingly telling. It embraced the lives of the most diverse individuals: two soldiers, hidden behind a pillar, taking it in turns to drink from a bottle; an old man who, for want of a seat, was sleeping on a newspaper spread out along one wall; a young mother whose face seemed as if it were glowing slightly, lit by an invisible candle; a prostitute watching at a snow-covered window; and a great many others.

Marooned there amid my fellow human beings,

some sleeping, some wakeful, I was marvelling privately at the philosopher's perspicacity ... And it was at that very moment, in the depths of a night cut off from the rest of the world, that the encounter took place.

A quarter of a century has passed since then. The empire whose fragmentation was predicted has collapsed. Barbarism and evil have manifested themselves under other skies too. And the formula invented by the Munich philosopher, who was, of course, Alexander Zinoviev, the defining phrase, almost forgotten today, simply serves me as a marker, signposting the moment of that brief encounter in the muddy tide of the years.

I have just woken up, having dreamed of music. The final chord fades away within me while I try to focus on individuals amid the living, breathing mass packed into this vast waiting-room in this mixture of sleep and weariness.

A woman's face, there, close by the window. Her body has just been pleasuring yet another man, her eyes are searching among the passengers for her next lover. A railwayman comes in quickly, crosses the room, departs through the big door that leads out onto the platforms, onto the night. Before closing, the door hurls a violent flurry of snow into the room. The people settled near the exit stir on their hard, narrow bench, tug on their coat collars, shake their shoulders with a shiver. From the other end of the station comes a muffled shout of laughter, then the crunch of a fragment of glass under a foot, an oath. Two soldiers, their *shapkas* pushed back on their heads, their greatcoats unbuttoned, beat a path through the mass of huddled bodies. Snores call out to one another, some of them in comic harmony. The wail of an infant rings out very clearly in the darkness, fades into little whimperings as it sucks, falls silent. A long argument, dulled by boredom, is taking place behind one of the pillars that hold up a varnished wooden gallery. The loudspeaker on the wall crackles, hisses and suddenly announces, in astonishingly soothing tones, that a train is going to be delayed. An ocean swell of sighs ripples through the waiting-room. But the truth is that no one expects anything any more. 'Six hours' delay . . .' It could be six days or six weeks. Numbness returns. The wind whips heavy white squalls against the windows. Bodies settle down against the hardness of the benches, strangers press close together, like the scales of a single protective shell. Night fuses the sleepers into one living mass – a beast savouring, with every cell in its body, its good fortune at being under cover.

From my position I can hardly see the clock that hangs above the ticket office. I turn my wrist, the dial of my watch catches the glow from the night-light: a quarter to one. The prostitute is still at her post, her silhouette stands out against the window made blue by the snow. She is not tall, but very broad in the hips. She towers above the ranks of sleeping travellers: it looks like a battlefield strewn with dead . . . The door leading to the town opens, new arrivals come in, bringing with them the cold and discomfort of open spaces scoured by snow flurries. The human protoplasm shivers and grudgingly makes space for these new cells.

I shake myself in an attempt to wrest myself away

from this conglomeration of bodies. To wrest those immediately around me from the blur of the whole mass. The old man, newly arrived, who lays no claim to a seat in this crowded station and unfolds a newspaper across the tiled floor, all filthy with cigarette ends and melted snow, before lying down, his back to the wall. The woman whose features and age are concealed by her shawl, an unknowable being swathed in a huge, shapeless coat. A moment earlier she was talking in her sleep: a few pleading words, that doubtless surfaced from years long ago in her life. 'The only clue to her humanity I'll ever have,' I tell myself. This other woman, this young mother, bowed over the cocoon of her baby, which she seems to envelop in an invisible halo made up of anxiety, wonder and love. A few steps away from her the prostitute, busy negotiating with the soldiers: the two men's excited jabbering and her whispering, a little disdainful but warm and as if moist with luscious promise. The soldiers' boots clatter on the flagstones; one can sense, physically, the eagerness her body provokes, with its broad, heavy backside and thrusting bosom under the coat . . . And there, almost on a level with the boots, the face of a man asleep, partly slipped from his bench, his head thrown back, his mouth half open, one hand touching the ground. 'A dead man on a battlefield,' I say to myself again.

My efforts to salvage a few individual figures from the anonymity of the whole begin to flag. Everything merges in the darkness, in the murky, dirty yellow glow from the streetlamp outside, in the nothingness that extends as far as the eye can see around this town buried beneath a snowstorm. 'A town in the Urals,' I say to myself, trying to link this railway station to some place, some direction. But my geographical impulse turns out to be ludicrous. A black dot lost in a white ocean. The Ural mountains that stretch over a thousand (two thousand?) miles. This town somewhere in the middle of them and, over to the east, the endlessness of Siberia, the endlessness of that snow-hell. Instead of locating them, my mind mislays both the town and its station on a white, uninhabited planet. The shadowy beings around me on whom I have been focusing melt once more into a single mass. Their breathing blends together, the mutterings of nocturnal narratives are drowned by the wheezing sounds of sleep. The murmur of the lullaby, more recited than crooned by the young mother, reaches me simultaneously with the whispering of the soldiers as they follow hard on the prostitute's heels. The door closes behind them, a wave of cold sweeps through the room. The young mother's murmurings take shape as a faint mist. The man sleeping with his head thrown back utters a long groan, sits up abruptly on his bench, woken by the sound of his own voice, stares lengthily at the clock, goes back to sleep again.

I know that the time he has just read on its face meant nothing. Nor would he have evinced more surprise on discovering that a whole night had gone by. A night or a couple of nights. Or a month. Or a whole year. A snow-filled void. In the middle of nowhere. A night without end. A night discarded on the verge of time . . .

Suddenly this music! Sleep retreats like the undertow of a wave in which a child grasps at a half-glimpsed shell, as I do at this cluster of notes, just heard in a dream.

A sharper cold: the door has opened and closed twice. First, the soldiers coming in and disappearing into the darkness. Their sniggering can be heard. A few minutes later the prostitute . . . So I had dozed off for the duration of . . . of their absence. 'Of their couplings!' a voice exclaims within me, irritated by that mealy-mouthed 'absence'.

This is certainly a place to dream of music. I remember how at nightfall, when there was still a slight chance of my getting away again, I went out onto the platform, superstitiously calculating that I could will a train to arrive by scorning the cold. Bowed under the violence of the squalls, blinded by the volleys of snowflakes, I tramped along beside the station building, but hesitated to venture any further, so much did the far end of the platform already resemble a virgin plain. Then, noticing a faint rectangle of light in one of the outhouses swamped amid the dunes of snow, I started walking again, or rather swaying, as if on stilts, plunging in up to my knees, striving to place my feet in a set of now almost obliterated footprints that had followed the same course. The door beside the small lighted window was closed. I took several steps towards the tracks that were already invisible beneath the snow, hoping at least for a mirage – an engine headlamp in the white chaos of the storm. My only consolation, on turning my back to the wind, was recovering my vision. Thus it was that this man suddenly caught my eye. It looked as if he had been thrown out of the little outhouse. The door, blocked by the snow, had resisted him and in order to escape he must have flung himself against it with all his might. Several times perhaps. Eventually the door had given way and he had toppled out into the night, into the storm, his face buffeted by snow flurries, his eyes dazzled by the white flakes, losing all sense of direction. Disconcerted, it took him a moment to close the door again, as it dragged against a thick layer of snow. During these few seconds, while he was pushing at the door, I saw the inside of the little place. A kind of hallway flooded with bright light, lemon coloured from the bare bulb, and beyond it, a room. Framed by this inner doorway, I saw a flash of ponderous nakedness, the massive whiteness of a belly and, in particular, the rough gesture of a hand, that grasped first one breast, then another, vast breasts, worn out by brutal caresses, and thrust them into a brassiere . . . But almost at once, with a screech of panic, a woman had appeared on the threshold, muffled up in a padded jacket (the keeper of the storeroom, who rents it out as a trackside love nest, I said to myself), and the door had closed with an angry slam . . .

The human mass sleeps on. The only new sound is of munching in the darkness: the old man, stretched out on his newspaper, has propped himself up on one elbow, opened a tin of food and is lapping it up, as people do who have very few teeth left. The metallic clatter of the lid closing makes me wince at its grating ugliness. The man lies down, seeks a comfortable position, with much rustling of sheets of newspaper, and soon begins to snore.

The judgement I have been trying to keep at bay floods in on me, a combination of sympathy and rage. I contemplate this human matter, breathing like a single organism, its resignation, its innate disregard of comfort, its endurance in the face of the absurd. Six hours' delay. I turn and study the waiting-room plunged in darkness. The truth is they could all easily spend several more nights here. They could get used to living here! Just like this, on a spread-out newspaper, backed up against the radiator, with nothing but a tin of food for nourishment. The notion suddenly seems to me perfectly plausible. An all-too plausible nightmare. For in these small towns a thousand leagues from civilization this is what life consists of: waiting, resignation, hot stickiness in the depths of your shoes. And this station besieged by the snowstorm is nothing other than a microcosm of the whole country's history. Of its innermost character. The vast spaces that render any attempt at action absurd. The superabundance of space that swallows up time, that equalizes all delays, all lapses of time, all plans. 'Tomorrow' means 'one day, perhaps'. One day, when the space, the snows and destiny allow it. Fatalism . . .

Mainly from vexation, I take a turn along the well-trodden paths of the national character, those accursed questions of Russian-ness that so many brilliant brains have grappled with. A land outside of History. The crushing inheritance of Byzantium. Two centuries of the Tartar yoke. Five centuries of serfdom. Revolutions. Stalin. 'East is East' . . .

After a few such laps round the circuit, the mind comes back to the dull geniality of the present day and lapses into helpless silence. These fine phrases explain everything and nothing. When confronted by the evidence of this night, this sleeping mass, with its smell of wet overcoats, weary bodies, alcohol fumes and warm tinned food, they fade away. For how can one sit in judgement on this old man as he lies there on his spread-out newspaper, a human being touching in his resignation, and quite insufferable for the same reason, a man who has doubtless lived through the empire's two great wars, survived the purges, the famines, but who nevertheless thinks he deserves nothing better than this resting-place on a floor covered in spittle and cigarette ends? Or the young mother who has just metamorphosed from Madonna into wooden idol, with slanting eyes and the features of a Buddha? If I woke them and asked them about their lives they would unflinchingly declare that the country where they lived was, give or take a few delayed trains, a paradise. And if in steely tones the loudspeaker were suddenly to announce the outbreak of war, the whole mass of them would set off, ready to endure the war as a matter of course, ready to suffer, ready to sacrifice themselves, with an utterly natural acceptance of hunger, of death, or of life in the filth of this station, here amid the cold of the great plains that stretch out beyond the tracks.

I tell myself there is a name for such a mentality. A term I have recently heard on the lips of a friend who listens in secret to western radio stations. A formula I have on the tip of my tongue, that only fatigue prevents me from calling to mind. I pull myself together and the phrase, luminous and definitive, bursts forth: '*Homo sovieticus!*'

The force of it pins down the whole impenetrable collection of lives around me. '*Homo sovieticus*' covers this human stagnation, down to its tiniest sigh, down to the clink of a bottle against the edge of a glass, down to the pages of *Pravda* under the scrawny body of the old man in his worn overcoat, pages filled with stories of targets achieved and perfect bliss.

With puerile delight I spend a moment playing with it: this phrase, a veritable key phrase, slips readily into all the keyholes of the country's existence, unlocking the secrets of all lives. Even the secret of love, such as it is lived in this country, with its official puritanism on the one hand, while a few yards away from those great panels with their images of Lenin and their edifying slogans this prostitute plies her trade – an almost licensed contraband.

Before falling asleep I have time to note that my command of this magic phrase sets me apart from the crowd. I am like them, certainly, but I can put a name to our human condition and therefore escape from it. The frail reed, that knows what it is and therefore . . . 'Hah, that old hypocritical device of the intelligentsia . . .' a more lucid voice whispers within me, but the mental comfort afforded me by '*Homo sovieticus*' quickly silences this objection.

The music! On this occasion I have enough time to catch the reverberation of the last notes, like a silken thread emerging from a needle's eye. I remain motionless for a few moments, listening for a fresh sound amid the torpor of the sleeping bodies. Now I know I was not dreaming; I have even more or less grasped where the music was coming from. All it was, in any case, was the brief stirrings of a keyboard, very spaced out, muted by the clutter in the corridors, muffled by the snoring.

I look at my watch: half-past three. Even more than the time and place at which this music has emerged, what surprises me is its detachment. It renders my philosophical rage of a few minutes ago perfectly futile. Its beauty does not invite one to flee the smell of tinned food and alcohol that hangs over the mass of sleepers. It simply marks a frontier, evokes a different order of things. Suddenly everything is illuminated by a truth that has no need of words: this night lost in a void of snow; a good hundred travellers huddled here; each seems as if he were breathing gently upon the fragile spark of his own life; this station with its vanished platforms; and these notes stealing in like moments from an utterly different night.

I get up, cross the waiting-room and climb the old wooden staircase. Feeling my way, I come to the bay window of the restaurant. The darkness is complete. Running my hand along the wall, I reach a dead-end, stumble over a pile of sleeping-car blankets, decide to abandon my investigation. A very slow chord resounds lingeringly at the other end of the corridor. I make my way towards it, guided by the fading sound, push open a door and find myself in a passage into which a little light now filters. Lined up along the walls stand banners, placards with portraits of the Party leaders, all the apparatus for demonstrations. The passageway leads to a room that is yet more cluttered. Two wardrobes with open doors, pyramids of chairs, piles of sheets. From behind the wardrobes shines a beam of light. I move forward, feeling as if I had caught up with the tail-end of a dream and were taking my place in it. A man, whom I see in profile, is sitting at a grand piano. A suitcase with nickel-plated corners stands beside his chair. It would be easy to mistake him for the old man sleeping on the pages of his *Pravda*. He is dressed in a similar overcoat, longer perhaps, and wearing an identical black *shapka*. An electric torch laid to the left of the keyboard throws light on the man's hands. He has fingers that are nothing like a musician's fingers. Great, rough, lumpy knuckles, tanned and wrinkled. The fingers move about on the keyboard without depressing the keys, pausing, springing to life, accelerating their silent course, getting carried away in a feverish flight: one can hear the fingernails tapping on the wooden keys. Suddenly, at the very height of this mute pandemonium, one hand loses control, crashes down on the keyboard, a shower of notes bursts forth. I see that the man, doubtless amused by his own clumsiness, breaks off from his soundless scales and begins emitting little suppressed chuckles, the quiet mirth of a mischievous old man. He even raises one hand and presses it to his mouth to restrain these splutters of laughter . . . All at once I realize he is weeping.

I withdraw with awkward, hesitant steps, one hand behind my back, feeling for the door. Just as I am close to the exit, my foot catches against a flagpole which falls, bringing a whole string of portraits on their long staffs toppling down in a noisy chain reaction . . . The beam from the electric torch sweeps along the wall and dazzles me. The man at once lowers it towards my feet, as if to apologize for having blinded me. A moment's embarrassed silence gives me the chance to notice the deep groove of a scar, whitened with age, across his brow, and his tears. 'I was just looking for a chair,' I stammer, glancing away. 'It's absolutely packed downstairs . . .'

The man switches off his torch and in the darkness I hear his words and, in particular, a brief rubbing sound from which I can deduce his gesture: he is swiftly wiping his eyes with the sleeve of his overcoat.

'Oh well, if it's a chair you're after, there's all you could want up here. Only take care, most of them have broken legs. Now, I've got a whole divan to myself – mind you, several of the springs are coming through . . .'

I notice that the darkness in this room is not total.

There are two windows that stand out in the blackness, illuminated by a streetlamp, and by the unremitting tornadoes of snow whirling about in the beam of light. I see the silhouette of the man as he makes his way round the wardrobes and disappears into a corner from which comes the shrill creak of springs.

'If they happen to announce a train, please wake me up,' he says from his divan.

And he wishes me a good night. I pull up a chair and settle down amid the scattered portraits, resolved to maintain to the end the pretence that I had just come looking for a chair and had not caught sight of his tears . . .

I pretend so well that I very quickly fall asleep, overcome by that deep slumber of the small hours that follows a sleepless night. It is the pianist who wakes me, his hand on my shoulder, the little torch throwing shadows onto the wall cast by tangled chairs, a suitcase, the open lid of the piano . . .

'They've just announced the Moscow train! If it's yours you'd better hurry. It'll be the storming of the Bastille out there.'

He is right. It is an assault. A mad scramble of faces, with huge suitcases shuttling back and forth, shouting and the tramp of feet along trenches excavated through the deep snow on the platforms. In the midst of this jostling I quickly lose sight of the man who has just woken me. A ticket inspector stops me in my tracks on the steps of the carriage where I was about to climb in. 'They're already packed in there like sardines. Can't you see?' The door to the next one is bolted. Around the third is gathered a crowd from which a hubbub arises, alternately wheedling and menacing. The inspector checks tickets, admitting occasional lucky ones, according to criteria it appears even he would find hard to explain. Stumbling in the snow pitted with footprints, I rush down the length of the train. An old woman stuck in a snowdrift bewails the fact that she has dropped her glasses. A soldier, on his knees, digs in the snow like a dog. A few yards from there his comrade urinates against a lamppost. The first one fishes out the glasses with a long string of triumphant oaths . . .

I tramp from one coach to the next, increasingly convinced I shall have to spend yet another day trapped in this town. My verdict of the night before returns, reanimated by the cold and my rage: '*Homo sovieticus!* That says it all. At this point you could tell them to climb onto the carriage roofs or, worse still, run behind the train, and not one of them would complain . . . *Homo sovieticus!*'

Suddenly this whistle. Not the whistle of the train. A short, street urchin's whistle, a piercing, peremptory summons, intended for an accomplice. I raise my head above the crowd besieging the carriage steps. At the end of the train I see the pianist waving his arm.

'They sometimes add one on, especially when there's a hold-up like this,' he explains to me as we settle into an ancient third-class coach. 'We shan't be warm, but, you'll see, the tea's even better here . . .'

Which is more or less all he says to me throughout the day. His nocturnal recital already hardly seems real to me. In any case, questioning him about that silent music would be to admit that I had seen him weeping. So . . . stretched out on the bare wooden couchette, I fall to conjuring up images of the human caravanserai I had observed camped in the waiting-room that night, now living through a fabulous experience without paying the least attention to it: the transit from Asia into Europe! Europe . . . Outside the window, in the small rectangle left clear by the hoar-frost, what rushes past is always the same infinity of snow, as far as the eye can see, impassive before the breathless advance of the train. The white undulation of the forests. An icebound river, immense, grey, reminiscent of an arm of sea. And once more the sleep of the white, uninhabited planet. I turn slightly, I study the old man, motionless on the opposite couchette, his eyes closed, his fingers interlaced on his chest. Fingers that know how to play silent melodies. Is he thinking of Europe? Is he aware that we are approaching civilization, cities where time can offer the stimulation of social inter-course, meetings, the exchange of ideas? Where space is tamed by architecture, curved inwards by the speed of a motorway, humanized by the smile of a caryatid whose face can be seen from the window of my flat, not far from the Nevsky Prospekt?

Curiously enough, it is on the subject of the beauty of certain streets that our conversation finally takes off, when it is already nearly evening. We have just pulled out of a large city on the Volga. The train has been reorganized and for a moment I was even afraid we might be abandoned on a siding. There is plenty of room here, as if people scorned to enter this archaic third-class carriage.

My companion gets up, fetches two glasses of tea. On learning that I know Moscow well, he becomes animated, talks to me about the capital with an unexpected precision, with a fondness for this street or that metro station. 'It's the fondness of a provincial, who has lived in the capital,' I say to myself, 'and who likes impressing the people he's talking to with the originality of his personal guided tour.' But the more he talks, the more I become aware that his Moscow is quite an odd city, with obvious gaps, with little networks of streets where my memory sees only broad avenues and esplanades. More attentive now, I notice several hiatuses in his narrative which the man attempts to avoid, now by breaking off in mid-sentence, now by telling an anecdote. 'Before the war . . .', 'During the thirties . . .'; these traces of the past slip out and suggest to me that he is strolling through a city that no longer exists. In the end he becomes aware of this, falls silent. At this moment of embarrassment his ear must have detected the same discordant tonality as last night, when I came upon him at the piano. To change the subject, I begin cursing the weather and the delays that will make me miss my connection in Moscow. We prepare our supper: hard-boiled eggs that I take out of my bag, the bread he says he has in his case. He extracts a parcel, unwraps it. Half a loaf of black bread. But it is the wrapping that catches my eye – crumpled pages of old sheet music. He looks up at me, then begins smoothing the pages with the rough edge of his hand. He no longer speaks in the tones of a sentimental traveller as he did a moment ago. And yet he is still talking about the same narrow Moscow streets – and about a young man ('In those days I counted myself the happiest man in the world,' he says with a bitter smile), a young man wearing a pale shirt soaked by a late spring shower, a young man stopping in front of a poster and reading his name with a beating heart: Alexeï Berg.

P reviously it was the name of his father, a playwright, that he used to look out for on such posters, and also, from time to time, that of his mother, Victoria Berg, when she was giving recitals. On that day, for the first time, it was his own name that was advertised. His first concert, a week hence, 24 May 1941.

The shower of rain had made the paper almost transparent so that the previous poster (for a parachute-jumping competition) showed through. And the picture of Tchaikovsky, all crinkled, looked like that of a court jester. Furthermore the concert was to take place at the ball-bearing factory's house of culture. But none of this could spoil his pleasure. The delight over which this waterlogged blue sheet cast its glow was much more complex than simple pride. There was the joy of the damp, luminous evening, emerging, as the storm abated, with all the freshness of a picture printed from a transfer. And the smell of foliage dusted with sun-drenched raindrops. The joy of streets darkened by rain, along which he strolled absent-mindedly, making his way back from the outskirts of the city, where the house of culture was situated, towards the centre. Even the auditorium where he was due to perform, an auditorium whose walls were covered in photos of machine tools and whose acoustics left much to be desired, had seemed to him festive and airy.

That evening Moscow was airy. Light beneath his tread in the network of little streets he knew by heart. Light and fluid in his thoughts. Pausing for a moment on the Stone Bridge, he looked at the Kremlin. The restless, grey-blue sky lent an unstable, almost dancing air to the cluster of domes and battlements. And to the left of it the view toppled over into the immense void left by the cathedral of Christ-the-Saviour, dynamited several years before.

Several years . . . As he resumed his walk Alexeï tried to recall the sequence of those years. The cathedral had been destroyed in 1934. He was fourteen. Fantastic excitement as he felt the pavement shuddering after each explosion! Those were the years of happiness. 1934, '35, '36 . . . Then suddenly this long quarantine descends, as it would during an epidemic. The city grows oppressive around their family. One evening, going up the stairs, he hears the whispering of a man one floor above him, climbing laboriously, absorbed in an almost inaudible but frenzied soliloquy. 'No, no, you can't accuse me . . . What proof do you have . . . ? What proof . . . ?' Alexeï hears these snatches, slows down, embarrassed to be eavesdropping like this, and suddenly recognizes his own father. This little old man muttering away is his father! . . . The quarantine lasts. Certain words can no longer be spoken. The *Dictionary of the Theatre*, published by his father at the beginning of the thirties, is withdrawn from all libraries. Certain names that he included in it have to disappear since the people who bore these names have recently disappeared. In class Alexeï notices rapid chess moves being made: his fellow pupils change places so as not to sit next to him. 'They're castling,' he thinks bitterly. At the school gates they move away from him, bobbing and weaving as they take off, like skiers on a descent strewn with obstacles. At the Conservatoire it seems as if the people he passes have all become short-sighted, they squint to avoid catching his eye. Their faces remind him of those masks he once saw in a history book, terrifying masks with long noses, with which the inhabitants of cities invaded by the plague used to rig themselves out. His friends acknowledge his greetings but obliquely, furtively, turning their heads away, and this evasive action – half in profile, half face on – stretches out their noses into the long incurved stings of insects. They stammer out excuses for making off and gasp as if they were inhaling the aromatic herbs that used to be stuffed into those anti-plague masks . . . During the winter of '39, he overhears his parents deliberating in secret, then, in the middle of the night, sees them putting their plan into action. They burn his father's old violin in the kitchen stove. On two or three occasions Marshal Tukhachevsky, a friend of the family and a good violinist, had played on it for their guests after dinner. He is executed in '37 and the little violin with its cracked varnish becomes a terrible piece of incriminating evidence . . . That night they burn it, fearing arrest and interrogation. In his panic his father forgets to loosen the strings and, lurking behind the half-open door of his bedroom, Alexeï hears the swift arpeggio of the strings snapping in the fire . . . From that night onwards they begin to breathe more freely. One of his father's plays is staged again. Still very occasionally, his mother's name reappears on posters. During 1940 an increasing number of people look Alexeï straight in the eye. As if thanks to some kind of ophthalmic miracle cure. He celebrates the new year in the company of these sham myopes. One of the tangos they dance to that night is called 'Velvet Glances'. After the years of fear and humiliation, he has a shrewd idea what this 'velvety' languor and the glances of the girls he holds in his arms are really worth. But he is only twenty-one and has a dizzying backlog of tangos, embraces, and kisses to catch up on. And he is fiercely determined to catch up on it, even if it were to mean forgetting that night, the smell of burning varnish, and the brief moaning of the strings in the flames.

He moved away from the Kremlin, diving in under the rain-bowed branches along the boulevards. The business with the violin, the nocturnal terror, his years of loneliness as a plague victim, still came back to him from time to time, but mainly to give a keen edge to the happiness he now enjoyed. His parents whispering in the night, the acrid smell of burning varnish, this was the only residue of those three black years, '37, '38, '39. Trifling matters beside the many varied pleasures that had filled his life since then. Why, just the wet shirt clinging to his chest and the simple delight he took in the feel of his young, supple, muscular body banished all the anguish of those epidemic years. But, above all, his concert, in a week's time, and his parents, whom he pictured seated at the back of the hall (he had fiercely negotiated their incognito attendance), and, in the front row, one of those girls with whom, on New Year's Eve, he had danced to 'Velvet Glances'. Lera.

The image of a transfer struck him once more . . . The whole world bore a resemblance to this trick with colours: all you had to do was peel back a thin, greyish membrane of unhappy memories and joy shone forth.

Just as, at the beginning of May, Lera's nakedness had shone forth from beneath that brown dress they had torn off together in the haste of still secret kisses, their ears cocked towards the sounds in the corridor of the *dacha*: her father, an elderly physicist, was working on the verandah and from time to time would call for a cup of tea or a cushion. Hers was a very wholesome nakedness, one of those bodies such as could be seen at that time, marching along dressed in flimsy singlets, in parades to the glory of youth. What Lera said was also very wholesome. She talked about a family, the flat they would live in, children. Alexeï sensed that this marriage would at last make him just like the others, banishing the figure of that youth secretly listening to the notes of the violin strings consumed in the fire. His own dreams, if the truth be told, were less of that young family nest and more of his father's car, the broad, black Emka, as comfortable as a luxury cabin on an ocean liner, which he already knew how to drive. To put that frightened adolescent behind him once and for all, it sufficed for him to picture that car, himself, Lera, and the blue line of the forest on the horizon.

His thoughts slid on to the days spent at the *dacha*, in that village with the melodious name of Bor. To the peeling back of the transfer as that body emerges from the schoolgirl's dress and abandons itself to the boldest of caresses, to a carnal struggle, to that laughing violence from which they both emerge breathless, their vision blurred by tears of pent-up desire. At the last moment the young body shies away, closing in on itself like a shellfish, over its virginity. And this manoeuvre pleases Alexeï. In her resistance he reads a commitment to future fidelity, the promise of a responsible and sensible young woman. Only once does doubt arise. Waking in a sunlit room after a brief sleep, through his eyelashes he sees Lera, already up, at the door. She turns and, believing he is still asleep, throws a glance at him that makes his blood run cold. It reminds him of the looks the long-nosed masks used to give him. To banish this resemblance, he leaps up, catches Lera on the threshold and drags her back towards the bed in a battle that is a mixture of laughter, love bites and attempts to break free. When she finally manages to escape he feels not the exhilaration of happiness but a sudden weariness, as at the end of a drama he has been forced to act out. And he senses that this female body, simultaneously offered and forbidden, this smooth, full body belongs to a life that will never be his. Oh yes it will, he corrects himself at once, he will marry Lera and their life will be made of the same stuff as this spring afternoon. One thing, though, he must forget the melody of the violin strings snapping in the fire. The life they are to lead will have the ring of music composed for a march past in a sports stadium. He remembers how one day he tried to tell Lera about those notes escaping from the strings as they burned. She interrupted him with just this enthusiastic advice: 'Why don't you write a march for sports parades . . . ?'

In the courtyard in front of the block of flats he could not avoid a brief stab of anxiety: 'The Battleships game!' One day, during the years of the terror, that was how all the windows in this façade – with those belonging to their own flat right in the middle – had appeared to him: squares on a sheet of paper struck through by an invisible – unforeseeable! – hand, as it hurled the occupants into a black car that arrived towards the end of the night and drove off again with its prey. Next morning they would learn that this or that flat was now empty. 'Hit and sunk . . .'

His gaze slid along to those three windows, three squares untouched amid so many vessels sunk. The old fear was gone. His present happiness was too intense to leave room for it. Alexeï only regretted one thing: a very important phase of his life had been surgically removed by those accursed years, one that he would have found hard to define. The time of youth's first flush, an age of dreaming and exaltation, when one poeticizes woman, making a divinity of her inaccessible flesh, living in wild anticipation of the miracle of love. None of all that for him. He had the impression that, in one sudden leap, he had been catapulted from childhood, from that pavement shaking with the destruction of the dynamited cathedral, right over the years of terror – into an already adult life, to face the nakedness of the beautiful, muscular body Lera offered him almost in its entirety, reserving that little 'almost' for marriage.

He went up the stairs, and on each landing noted the number of departures and arrivals that had occurred, especially when the Battleships game was at its height in '37, '38, '39. People dragged from their sleep, experiencing their departure as a dream that skidded into horror. There was the flat beneath their own: a family, a little girl who had met him in the street only a few days before their noctural departure and talked to him about a new flavour of ice cream they were selling on the boulevards . . .

He quickened his step and began singing an operatic aria from his mother's repertoire, a love song replete with heady, smouldering key changes. She heard him through the door and, smiling, came to open it.

Two days before the concert he went back to the factory's house of culture for the final rehearsal. 'The dress rehearsal', as he had announced it to his parents during lunch. He worked all afternoon, played through the entire programme and then stopped, remembering his mother's advice: sometimes by dint of rehearsing the intimate thrill of novelty can be lost, the tiny element of miracle or conjuring trick that art cannot do without. 'You know, it's like stage fright,' she added. 'If you don't have it at all it's a bad sign . . .'

On the way home he was thinking about this beneficial fear, the shiver that spurs one on. It had been lacking that time, during the rehearsal. 'Yes, but playing in a steam bath like that . . .' he excused himself. It was a heavy, hot, milky day. A day with no colour, no life in it. 'No stage fright in it,' he said to himself, smiling. His mother had also told him about young actresses who claimed they never had stage fright, and to whom Sarah Bernhardt, ironically indulgent, would promise: 'Wait a little. That will come with talent . . .'

Even beneath the greenery of the boulevards the muggy torpor hung there stagnating, muffling sounds, swathing the trees, the benches, the lampposts in a grey light; that of a day already lived through once before and now seemingly stumbled into by mistake. Alexeï was leaving the main avenue to take a short cut when suddenly a figure he at once recognized emerged from a row of trees: a neighbour of theirs, a retired man who could often be seen sitting in the courtyard, bent over a chessboard. Just now he was advancing with a hurried and oddly mechanical gait, coming straight towards him and yet seeming not to have noticed him. Alexeï was already preparing to greet him, to shake his hand, but, without looking at him, without slowing down, the man walked straight past. At the very last moment of this abortive encounter, however, the old man's lips moved slightly. Very softly but quite distinctly, he breathed: 'Don't go home.' And he walked on faster, turning off into a narrow sidestreet.

Taken aback, Alexeï remained perplexed for a moment, not believing his ears, unable even to grasp what he had just heard. Then he rushed after the old man, caught up with him near a crossroads. But before he could ask him for an explanation the neighbour, still avoiding his eye, whispered: 'Don't go back. Run for it. Things are bad over there.' And, with the red light against him, the old man scuttled across in front of a car, which hooted. Alexeï did not follow. In the

34

face turned away from him he had just caught sight of the long-nosed mask.

Pulling himself together, he realized the extent to which the old man's words were absurd. 'Things are bad over there.' Sheer madness. An accident? An illness? He thought of his parents. But then why not say so clearly?

He hesitated, then, instead of going directly into the courtyard, walked round the whole block of dwellings and went up into the building where the stairwell had windows with a view across to the façade of their house. On the top landing there were no flats, just the exit leading out under the roofs. He knew this observation post as it was where he had smoked his first cigarette. There was even a lingering presence of that vaguely criminal feeling. Through a narrow fanlight he could see the whole courtyard, the bench where the retired folk read their newspapers or played chess, and if he pressed his brow against the panes of glass he could make out the windows to his parents' bedroom and the kitchen. And as he peered across, the taste of the first puffs of tobacco came floating back.

He spent a long while with his face pressed to the glass. The façade of the building was familiar to him down to the smallest cornice, down to the designs on the curtains at the windows. The foliage of a lime tree that reached almost to the level of their flat hung there, motionless in the dull heat of the

evening, as if waiting for a sign. For a May evening
there were surprisingly few people in the courtyard.
Those who crossed it slipped along noiselessly and
disappeared swiftly into the drowsiness of the alleys.
Even the stairwell remained silent, no one seemed to
be entering or leaving. The only sound: the creaking
of a little bicycle on which a child was pedalling
tirelessly round a bed of campanulas. At one point
he stopped, looked up. Alexeï shivered, moved away
from the fanlight. It felt as if the boy were directing a
precise, hard gaze at him, an adult's gaze. A sly little
adult on his bicycle.

The creaking of the wheels began again. Alexeï
decided his fear was stupid. Just as stupid as this
waiting behind a dusty pane of glass, just as stupid as
the old chess player's warning: he must have mistaken
him for someone else.

He had an impulse to go down quickly, to return
home in order to steal a march on his fear. 'Stage
fright,' he giggled silently and began pounding down
the staircase. But two floors below he stopped. A
couple had just come in and were on their way up,
forcing him to retreat to his refuge. He studied the
windows of the flat once more, as well as those of their
neighbours on the floor below. Suddenly he realized
what was keeping him here . . .

During the years of the terror that flat had witnessed
three departures. First of all they had taken away the
aircraft manufacturer and his family. Rumour in the

courtyard had it that it was his assistant who had denounced him in order to have his job and this flat. He had moved in there with his family, had just had time to buy new furniture for the dining-room and to feel they were a permanent fixture. Six months later, the night when their turn came, people heard the wails of their child, still half asleep, crying out for its favourite doll, which in the haste of the arrest no one had thought to take with them. A week later a man moved in who wore the uniform of the Commissariat for State Security. When he passed his neighbours on the staircase, he stopped and stared at them obstinately, waiting for them to greet him. And his son looked like a young boar. At all events, it was with that animal's brutish violence that he had one day pushed Alexeï up against the wall and muttered between clenched teeth: 'So, rotten intelligentsia. Still banging away on our stinking little piano, are we? Well just you wait. One day I'm going to take a hammer and nail down the lid on your music!' Alexeï had said nothing about it to his parents. And in fact shortly after that, towards the end of 1938, the flat was emptied yet again . . .

He pressed his forehead against the glass. The curtains in his parents' flat seemed to be moving. No, nothing. His mind went back to that young boar-man, his bulging face, his scorn. And especially to his threat, quite fanciful, of course, but one that had often seemed very real: the piano, its lid nailed down with great carpenter's nails. In fact if he was now watching at this fanlight covered in cobwebs, it was because of that young boar. Thanks to the man's disappearance one December night, he had realized no one was safe. Not even the victors. Not even those who had fought valiantly against the enemies of the people. Not even these fighters' children.

At this moment he saw the chess player crossing the courtyard with a measured tread. The old man raised his arm in greeting to a woman watering the flowers at her window, then disappeared through an entrance door. The dusk was already making it impossible to see the expressions on people's faces. And, as if in response to this perception, the light came on, lending a glow of colour to his parents' bedroom curtains. A shadow appeared, very familiar. He was sure it was his mother. He even caught sight of a hand, her hand, of course, tugging at the curtains. 'I'm an absolute cretin and the worst kind of coward,' he said to himself, feeling a marvellous sense of relief in his chest. His gaze now slipped smoothly along the rows of windows that were beginning to light up. Peaceful, almost sleep-inducing in the calm of a May evening. Down below, in the building where he had taken refuge, a door slammed. The click of a lock, voices, silence. He decided to wait for one more minute, but this was now merely to avoid inquisitive glances. 'And besides, I've got my concert on Saturday . . .' a confident voice affirmed within him. This argument seemed to banish once and for all the danger invented by the old madman he had passed on the boulevards. 'I'll go home. I should be able to practise for an hour before the neighbours start kicking up a fuss.'

He took one last look at the block of flats and it was with this glance, already careless and wearied by the tension, that, through the dimness of their kitchen window, he saw a uniformed officer staring down at the courtyard.

It seemed to him as if the staircase would never come to an end. Rounding corner after corner in a frenzied gallop, he followed the zigzags of the handrails that continued interminably, as if by an optical illusion. In the streets, then in the corridors of the metro, and at the station, he still felt as if he were thrusting downwards in the murky spiral of that stairwell, dodging past doors that threatened to open at any moment. And his eyes carried with them the vision of a window where the figure of a man clad in a shoulder belt stood clearly silhouetted. He was not running, he was falling.

His fall came to a halt at the ticket windows. The woman in the ticket office extracted a little pink sphere from a box of sweets and popped it into her mouth. And even while her fingers were taking the money and handing over the change, her lips were moving, pressing the sweetmeat against her teeth. Alexeï stared at her in blank amazement: so beyond the glass flap of the ticket window an almost magical world began, made up of this wonderful routine of sweets, and yawning smiles. A world from which he had just been cast out.

He was so struck by the way this life went on serenely without him that he was not surprised at what happened in Bor at the *dacha*. Lera's father, the professor, generally cloistered in his study and deaf to all shouting and bells ringing, on this occasion opened the door to him almost immediately. At eleven o'clock at night. Nor did Alexeï find it surprising that the old man hardly listened to him, in his haste to offer him a meal that seemed to be already waiting for him on the kitchen table. Furthermore, in response to his attempts to explain what was happening to his parents, all the professor could say was: 'Eat up, eat up! Then try to get some sleep. The night brings good counsel.' He repeated this wise saying abstractedly several times, as if he were reaching the end of a train of thought which the young man's visit had interrupted.

Strangely enough, despite the fever that shook him,

Alexeï sank rapidly into a brief, deep sleep. He sought concealment in it, hoping to wake up on the other side of the ticket window behind which that young woman had been sucking a sweet. He had a dream in which the window was located very low down, almost on the ground. This basement window had taken the place of the ticket woman's and you had to stoop to catch sight of the face at it: Lera's face. But an ambiguous Lera, revealed in an unmentionable activity. The old chess player was there too, seated on a rain-soaked bench. Alexeï was playing with him, setting down the pieces not on a chessboard but on the pages of an anatomical atlas, in which the pictures were obscurely connected with their game. And his sleep was permeated by a fear of not grasping these connections, though they were obvious to the old man. Finally there was the figure of his mother, reciting lines of verse and suddenly singing them in a voice so shrill and desperate that he awoke with a stifled cry in his throat.

He looked at his watch: half-past three. Outside the window the night was beginning to grow pale. Alexeï studied the room, the outlines of the furniture, and thought, almost calmly: 'But, of course. He's going to denounce me . . .' In a flash all the oddities he had ignored the evening before coalesced into an inescapable logic. The professor, who never went to bed late, had opened the door at the first ring, fully dressed. His wife, without whom he could not go anywhere, was absent. So was Lera. In the bedroom it was as if everything had been ready to receive a guest . . . 'No, he won't denounce me, he'll simply let them in . . .'

He jumped out of bed, dressed, fastened the catch on the door, climbed out through the window . . .

At the start of the path he and Lera generally took to go and bathe in a pool, he hesitated, turned towards an old shed behind the house, sat down on a chopping-log and decided to wait. And did not have to wait long. From the far end of the main street that divided this plot of *dachas* in two came the sound of an engine. The car stopped. In the still nocturnal silence he heard the sound of banging at the door, the whispering of men's voices and, more distinctly, in imploring tones, but striving to preserve his dignity, the professor's voice: 'Comrades, you promised me . . . He's a delicate young man. I beg you! I'm sure his parents . . .' Someone cut him off in irritated tones: 'Now listen, professor, don't interfere in what doesn't concern you! You'll speak when you're questioned . . .'

Hurling himself along the path, Alexeï heard the hammering coming from inside the house.

Much later, when he was well versed in the pitiless mania life has for playing at paradoxes, he would come to realize that in reality he owed his survival to the Germans. Ever since the month of April in that year of 1941, and even earlier, but more confusedly, people in Moscow had been talking about the impending threat from the West. On such occasions his mother's thoughts turned to her sister's family who lived in a remote village in the Ukraine. Poor relations, so to speak, and never invited to Moscow. They pictured them in their hamlet very close to the Polish border, exposed to the increasingly predictable war. 'But come now,' his father would interrupt her, 'our army will never let the Germans cross the frontier. And even if, by some remote chance, they managed to drop a few bombs, there'd be nothing to fear. I simply take the car, drive to your sister's and, quick as a wink, I bring them back to Moscow.' This scheme for an evacuation by car would come up again from time to time in their family evenings together.

Alexeï recollected it now when at about six in the morning, he reached the suburbs of Moscow on foot. His head buzzed with the names of fellow students at the Conservatoire who might come to his aid, names which, reviewed one by one, faded into uncertainty. Then he thought about this aunt in the Ukraine, remembered the plan for a journey by car and eagerly seized upon the idea before it came to seem too far-fetched.

The garage, some streets away from their block of flats, was squeezed up against the wall of a demolished monastery. At this hour the place was still deserted, the doors to the other garages closed. He stood on tiptoe, holding his breath as if catching a butterfly, and reached out with his hand towards a little cavity beneath the corrugated iron of the roof. His father, being absent-minded, often left the duplicate key there. His fingers fumbled feverishly in the depths of the hiding-place and suddenly touched metal.

He put two cans of petrol, kept in reserve, into the boot, and, before climbing into the driving seat, looked about him. His mind, drained by weariness and fear, came to life: the garage, with a dull light bulb in the ceiling, the smell of petrol, these objects his father had touched – the last glimpse of their old life?

Footsteps crunched on the gravel. Alexeï slipped in behind the wheel, his mind a blank once more, his heart in his mouth, his body ready to go through the familiar motions and propel the heavy black car against the half-open door . . . But the sounds outside resolved themselves into an unthreatening sequence: the clink of a bunch of keys, the creaking of hinges, departure.

Stopping at a crossroads, he realized that he had only once had occasion to drive outside Moscow: to take Lera to the *dacha* in Bor.

In the car he found a bundle of road-maps, including one of the region in the Ukraine where his aunt lived. There was a jacket and an old cap lying on the back seat. He put them on and later noticed how much this garb facilitated his passage at militia checkpoints. Thanks in particular to the cap, he looked like a chauffeur in a hurry to reach the home of a high-ranking person. And the further he got from Moscow the more the appearance of the big black car commanded respect.

At the end of the second day of his journey, on what was already a country lane, he met an old farm cart being driven by a young peasant who stared open-mouthed at this car appearing amid the fields. With a strong nasal accent, in a mixture of Russian and Ukrainian, he gave him directions. Alexeï was a dozen miles from his destination.

Before night fell he drove on further, then turned off, following a track that plunged into the forest, and stopped when a thick tree-trunk barred his way. He ate a whole loaf, bought in a small town he had passed through at midday, felt intoxicated by the food, and by the onset of sleep. The forest all about the car seemed endless. He wanted to look at the time, remind himself of the date, as if to have a buoy to cling to amid the ocean of branches and shadows. Lying on the back seat, he held up his arm to the light filtering through the leaves. It was only half-past eight in the evening. May 24 . . .

'My concert!' he breathed, sitting up suddenly. A beautiful moth was fluttering against the rear window, its wings covered in fine, mysterious calligraphy, leaving traces of pollen on the glass. And it was thus, as if through the thickness of the glass, that he pictured the hall, the lights on the stage, a young man walking towards the piano. For a moment, in a poignant fantasy, he watched the continuation of that life somewhere without him.

In the morning he left the forest on foot. And glanced behind him several times: the sun, still low, filled the interior of the abandoned car with a golden light; it looked like a car left there by a family who had spread out among the trees, to gather wild strawberries.

His aunt listened to him in silence, let him talk for a long time, repeating himself. She sensed that this was how he would get used to his new life. His uncle returned from the town about midday and was equally taciturn. Weeks later Alexeï would guess that behind this silent acceptance of his coming, and the danger of his coming, there doubtless lay an unspoken desire to make him understand: 'Now look, we're plain country folk. We welcome you with open arms. We've got no grudges against our own kin, who forgot all about us.' But at the time all he needed was to be able to tell them his story, to win approval, to be reassured that, in any event, even if he had stayed in Moscow, he could not have done anything for his parents. He also realized that, in a few swift moves, they were already preparing for his clandestine existence in that house. Their economy with words and actions reminded him that the epidemic of fear his own family had known in '37 had made its assault on these people much earlier. At the end of the twenties, from the time when collectivization began in that part of the world. They had lost their two children in the famine that followed it, and had hidden fugitives before.

It was in one such hiding-place that his uncle installed him. They went to a tiny hay barn and by the half-light coming in between the planks Alexeï saw it was an empty space, with no window and not the smallest corner for a person to hide in. Seeing his disconcerted look, his uncle smiled and explained softly: 'It's a suitcase with a false bottom.' He leaned on a plank that gave way and, peering in through the opening, Alexeï saw a kind of narrow passage between two wooden walls, scarcely more than eighteen inches wide, with a folding bunk, a shelf nailed to the wall, a bucket, a jug, a bowl. 'You'll have to get your Moscow nose used to the smell of muck,' his uncle added. 'I put it all around the shed just in case they come with a dog . . .'

Two days later his uncle announced to him, a little

awkwardly: 'I know this'll go hard with you, but . . . that car . . . We've got to drown her. I'll show you the place where we can shove her in.'

Alexeï rapidly learned to mould his body and his movements within the confined section between the walls. One day he managed to suspend his secret life in mid-gesture when a voice rang out on the other side of the planks, rebuking his uncle: 'He's not far away, your nephew. People have seen him. It's in your own interests to help us, before we find him ourselves in your loft . . .' The uncle, very calm, replied in a dull voice: 'This nephew of mine: I've never seen him in my life. If you find him, I'll be meeting him for the first time . . .' Alexeï remained frozen, a spoon close to his lips, not even daring to brush away a fly from his forehead.

In the middle of the night he would leave his hiding-place. He would get up, change, stretch his legs. The serenity of the fields, the sky, the stars seen through a heat haze, called on him to have faith, to take joy in life. They were all lying.

In the end he had studied the tiniest of the cracks between the planks, knew what field of vision each offered. This one, above the shelf, gave a view of a narrow section of the road that linked the village to the district capital. That other one, next to the bunk flap, cut across a fence of dry branches.

One day he saw a man asleep, drunk, at the foot of this fence, lying there as if felled by a rifle shot. The panels of his jacket were spread out in the dust of the road, his snores reached all the way to the barn. This slumped body expressed such a blithe indifference to what anyone might think of him, such a lack of constraint in this temporary death, such a physical oblivion, that Alexeï became aware of a violent jealousy. Or rather of a temptation: to lay hands on this snoring corpse, search him, rob him of his papers, disguise himself in his clothes, return to life under this stolen name . . .

The splinters in the wooden plank pricked his cheek. Alexeï stared at the drunkard as if this were a miraculous vision. The man was nothing like him, at least twice his age, red-haired, with a flat nose. But this notion of stealing an identity, unlikely as it seemed for the moment, took root in his memory.

It was through one of the cracks between the planks that he saw his uncle's cart driving off one evening: his uncle held the reins, his aunt sat amid the crates of vegetables they were going to sell in the Sunday market at the district capital.

That night the sound of horses' hooves invaded his sleep. 'Back already?' he thought in surprise, still only half awake. The clatter became louder, reminiscent of thunder. His shoulder was pressed against the planks of the wall, he could feel them vibrating. 'All these horses!' his dream whispered to him, teeming with herds that made the earth tremble as they galloped. And at once, shaking off the dream's deception, he jumped down from the bunk, leaned against the board of the hidden door, went out into the night and saw the horizon on fire. Now the successive waves of bombing assaults could be heard more distinctly, settling into a regular rhythm. Very low, skimming over the roofs of the village, came one aeroplane after another. It was like an aerobatic display. But already the road was filling with people making their escape. Alexeï hastened to slip back into his hiding-place. His field of vision, between two planks, allowed him to snatch a glimpse of a mother stumbling as she dragged two sleepy children behind her, an old woman whipping a cow. Then, more quickly, travelling in the opposite direction, soldiers colliding with the waves of fugitives. And less than an hour later the smoke and the drumming of bullets, chipping the loam off the walls, and then suddenly there was this roaring hulk that grazed the barn in passing, hacking to pieces with its tracks the vegetable patch his aunt had been watering only the day before.

He remained lying on the ground for a long while. The walls of his hiding-place had been pierced with bullets here and there. Gradually the gamut of sounds became simpler, less varied. Still a few cries, the grinding of tank tracks, a burst of gunfire, already distant. And in the end just the hissing of the fire. Alexeï peered through one of the spyholes drilled by the shooting. Near the fence, at the exact spot where two weeks earlier he had seen a sleeping drunkard, sprawled the body of a soldier, his bloodied face turned directly towards the sunrise, as if sunbathing.

It took him two days to find his man, his identity donor. His searches in the burned-out village had been fruitless. He had come upon several survivors and had had to make himself scarce. On the road he found mainly the bodies of women and children or of men who were too old.

At the end of his second day of walking he went down towards a river, and on the bank, at the entrance to a bridge demolished by shelling, saw a complete battlefield: dozens of soldiers to whom death had lent poses that were sometimes really banal, like the one of a body with its legs buckled beneath it, some-times touching, like that of a young infantryman, his hand outstretched in an orator's gesture. Hiding in the undergrowth, Alexeï waited, listening intently, but could hear no moaning. The evening was still light, the faces of the dead when he finally dared to approach them were exposed in defenceless simplicity. He noticed that there were no German soldiers; these had presumably been carried away by their own side.

He looked into eyes, often wide open, noted the colour of hair, the build. From time to time his fascination with death led him to forget the purpose of his search, he sank into a robot-like torpor, transforming himself into a hypnotic camera that focused on these truncated lives one after another. Then he took a grip on himself, resumed the search for his double. Hair colour, shape of the face, build.

Very close to the river he found a face similar to his own but the soldier's hair was dark brown, almost black. He said to himself that he could shave off his blond hair and that in the photo on an identity document this difference in colour would hardly be visible. With trembling fingers, he unbuttoned the soldier's tunic pocket, seized the little book embossed with a red star and hurriedly put it back again. In the photo the soldier did not look like him at all and his hair framed his face like a charcoal line.

Pausing close to another, he noted the similarity of their features. But he suddenly observed that the soldier's left ear had been cut to pieces by a bullet. He moved on quickly, realizing at once that such a wound in no way undermined the resemblance, but lacking the courage to go back to that bloodied head.

He discovered another dead man by chance when, to get rid of the stench that hung over the river, he went into the water up to his knees and began rinsing his face and neck. The soldier's body was half crushed under a beam of the collapsed bridge. All that could be seen was the blond oval of his head, one arm pressed against his chest. He went closer, leaned forward, surprised by the degree to which this unknown face resembled his own, seized the beam, thrust it aside . . . And started back: the soldier's eyes came to life and a rapid torrent of words whispered in plaintive relief poured forth from his lips. In German! Then a long spurt of blood. And once again the fixity of death.

Taking long strides, in an effort to avoid seeing again the faces he already knew, he left the riverbank. He tried neither to make excuses for this retreat nor to seek comfort by telling himself that perhaps somewhere else . . . He was drained of himself, contaminated by death, driven out of his own body by all the dead men he had been dressing in his clothes, as he slipped into theirs. He spoke in rhythm with his footsteps, eager to replenish himself with what he had been before . . . But suddenly stopped. Far away from the others, his head washed by the current of the stream, lay a soldier. The one he had been looking for.

Alexeï began to strip him with actions that belonged

to another, actions that were somewhat brutal and businesslike . . . Once dressed, he noted that the boots were too tight. He went back towards the bridge and, in the same state of detachment, removed another soldier's boots. The right boot resisted. He sat down, stared helplessly at the great body his efforts had disturbed, saw himself from outside, a young man in the midst of a beautiful summer's evening on the riverbank fringed with sand – and these scores of corpses. From time to time a fish would stir idly among the reeds, beating the water with a resounding slap . . . He stood up, seized the boot stuck to the leg, began shaking it, tugging at it savagely. He was unaware that for a while now, he had been weeping and talking to someone and even believing he could hear replies.

Continuing along the road, he grew calmer. In the middle of a night spent in an abandoned farm cart he woke up, struck a match, read the name of the soldier he now was. In the pocket of the tunic he found the photograph of a young woman and a postcard, folded in two, with a view of the Winter Palace.

He had a vivid picture of his first encounter with the soldiers among whom he would have to lose himself, get himself accepted, not betray himself. Questions, inspections, he thought. And suspicion.

No such encounter really took place. At the edge of an unknown town, amid streets noisy with gunfire, he was quite simply drawn into a disorderly stampede of soldiers in flight from an as yet invisible danger, falling and shooting, almost without taking aim, at a cloud of smoke down at the end of a long avenue.

He ran along with them, picked up a rifle, imitated their firing and even their panic, although he did not feel it himself at that moment, having had no time to take stock either of their exhaustion or the monstrousness of the force they were attempting to confront. When at nightfall an officer succeeded in mustering some remnants of the routed army, Alexeï noticed that the soldiers came from the most diverse units, companies that had been wiped out, decimated regiments. So he was like them. The only difference was that sometimes he was more afraid of letting slip his real name than of finding himself under fire. As a result of this fear, and the assiduity with which he copied the actions of the others during these first few weeks, he did not feel as if he was engaged in combat. And when he was finally able to relax the constantly taut string within him, he found himself in the skin of a veteran soldier, taciturn and respected for his nerve, a man among thousands like him, indistinguishable in the column as it trudged along a muddy road, heading towards the heart of the war.

During the first two years at the front, Alexeï received four or five letters addressed to the man whose name he bore. He did not reply and reflected that his lie was certainly giving several people the strength to hope, the energy to survive.

Moreover he had long ago learned that in war truth and falsehood, magnanimity and callousness, intelligence and naivety could not be so clearly told apart as in the life before. The memory of the corpses on the bank of a river often came back to him. But now the horror of those minutes revealed its obverse side: if the young man from Moscow he then was had not spent that time among the dead he would doubtless have been shattered, from the very first battles, by the sight of eviscerated bodies. The boot he had wrenched off that corpse had been like a cruel but necessary vaccination for him. Sometimes, in a judgement he did not admit to himself, it even seemed that, compared with the removal of that dead man's boot, all the carnage he was now witnessing was less hard to endure.

One day, when he was first wounded, he discovered another paradox. Having come among these soldiers to escape death, he was exposing himself to a much more certain death here than in a re-education colony, where they would have sent him after his parents' arrest. He would have been safer behind the barbed-wire of a camp than in possession of this lethal liberty.

Nor could he ever have believed that during one short week, at the time of his convalescence and with one arm still in a sling, in a hospital that echoed with the groans of the wounded, it was possible to love, to become attached to a woman, with the feeling of having always known these eyes, this rather gruff voice, this body. And above all, if in the days of his former life in Moscow a friend had spoken to him of such a love, Alexeï would have laughed in his face, perceiving nothing more in such a relationship than a few hasty couplings and dull silences between a nurse and a convalescent soldier, who had only their bodies to offer one another. He would have scoffed at all the ridiculous details, the trappings of a novel of rustic life: the untidy bouquet picked along a roadside with his one good hand, a pair of worn gilt earrings, the woman's fingers stained brown with tincture of iodine.

All these things featured during that week of

convalescence. There was the hospital which, while an offensive was being prepared, was living through several days of respite in anticipation of fresh train-loads of wounded. The heavy smell of blood and bruised flesh. This woman, fifteen years older than himself, who seemed to be once more noticing that seasons existed, that the warm breath of the earth and the foam of lilac were called spring, and that a man, this rather gauche soldier she had started talking to one day, could become very close to her, that they were becoming very close, in spite of herself, in spite of him, in spite of everything. And when he surprised her one evening, as she appeared on the path that led from the hospital to the *izba* where she lodged, he with his arm in a sling and holding that bunch of flowers, she felt her voice thawing out: 'It's the first time anyone has ever . . .' He did not let her finish, hastened to crack a joke, to make her laugh. Then fell silent and, right up to his departure a week later, sensed that but for his arm, which was still painful, he could have sated himself utterly on this woman's body, draining the cup of everything she gave him.

In the trenches this unassuaged hunger would return, but already more all-embracing; he yearned both for the dust of that path leading to the *izba* (he would have given all he had simply to be able to touch those warm ruts lit by the setting sun) and for the glistening of the raindrops trickling down from the roof after a brief nocturnal shower, catching the moon's brilliance as they fell. He realized he even had a longing now for the sharp smell of iodine that emanated from those rather rough hands, whose caress he still felt on his face. This smell withstood time better than the physical memory of her, as that came to be erased by the sight of so many lifeless bodies and by brief encounters with women who left him neither the memory of a face nor a talisman like tincture of iodine.

The fear of being unmasked returned only on those occasions when he had the luck – ill luck for him – to receive an award for bravery. The commission that decided these matters, especially if an Order was under consideration, would check the soldier's past, so as to avoid decorating a former convict or someone expelled from the Party. Alexeï had long ago learned to appear lacklustre and though he often led the way in assaults, he knew how to make himself scarce after the end of a battle, when the commanding officer was noting down the names of the bravest.

He did hear music occasionally, that of military bands, or sometimes, at halts on the march, the plaintive merriment of an accordion. On his guard against any upsurge of nostalgia, he noted that nothing of this kind swept through him, no special emotion that might have recalled his youth as a pianist.

As for pianos, he saw one in the Lithuanian town where his regiment's offensive got bogged down for a whole week. Their advance was hampered by a number of snipers who had all the crossroads in their sights and were killing officers in a precise, clinical selection process. One of the snipers was hidden in a block of flats with blown-out windows, on the ground floor of which the interior of a drawing-room could be glimpsed, with velvet armchairs and a grand piano. A hundred yards from there Alexeï lay stretched out in the entrance hall of a house and from time to time, for the space of a second, poked his lure out through the open door: a plywood oval surmounted by an officer's cap, with two cylinders cut from a tin can fixed to the middle of it. An officer looking through his field glasses, the sniper's favourite target. Alexeï kept sticking it out and snatching it back in again, sending a brief whistle to his two comrades who were watching the street from the top floor . . . The shot rang out at a moment when he was no longer expecting it, the manipulation of the lure having become a reflex action. The noise of rending plywood was drowned at once by bursts of gunfire from the top floor, then the thunder of boots on the staircase. 'We've got him!' shouted the soldier carrying a machine gun on his shoulder. The bullet had pierced the plywood just above the two tin circles. They examined the hole, touched it, laughed at it. Then went across the road to collect the German's rifle. Alexeï stopped beside the piano, let a hand come down on the keyboard, listened, closed the lid again. His joy at not feeling within himself the presence of a young man in love with music was very reassuring. He looked at his hand, the fingers covered in scars and scratches, the palm with its yellowish calluses. Another man's hand. In a book, he thought, a man in his situation would have rushed to the piano and played it, forgetting everything, weeping perhaps. He smiled. Such a thought, such a bookish notion, was probably the only link that still bound him to his past. Catching up with the soldiers, he encountered the lifeless stare of the German sniper lying on the floor and reflected that to this man he was just an incautious Russian officer allowing the lenses of his field glasses to glint. The plywood officer with eyes cut out of a tin can.

He hoped he could make his way through this war without adding any distinguishing marks to the identity of the man whose life he was now living. To be smooth, with no prominent features or personality, a little like that plywood oval. But in its whimsical way, which no longer surprised him, the war decided to make its own mark on the photo of the blond young man whom he so much resembled.

This was a second wound, much more serious than the previous one, and, after two weeks suspended between life and death, the first sight of himself in a mirror, at the moment when the dressing was being changed: a bare, ageless cranium, and a scar that ran aslant his brow from his hairline towards his temple.

He did everything possible to avoid being declared unfit for service. Pretended good health, despite the dull, persistent pain that permeated his whole being, despite the silence of death that had become lodged in his thoughts. The doctor spoke to him as if to a child trying to cling to its mother's hand when she has to go away: 'Listen, you're going to go and spend a month in your village. Mother's going to feed you up a bit, get some pies into you. And then we'll see.' Alexeï wanted to stay, not because of some spirit of heroic self-sacrifice but quite simply because he had nowhere to go.

The roads were still covered in ice: those early days of March saw little sunshine. He walked, sometimes rode on lorries, getting off in a village, telling the driver he lived there and continuing on foot. From time to time, pausing amid empty, white fields, amid all this land bruised by the war, he would sniff the air, believing he could detect something like a fleeting breath of warmth. He sensed that all the life that was left to him was concentrated in this faintly springlike breeze, in this airy, misty sunlight, in the scent of the waters awakening beneath the ice. And not in his emaciated body that no longer even felt the wind's scorching.

Confusedly, he realized that these roads, despite the detours, were leading him towards Moscow. Or rather towards a vague, nocturnal city, a place pictured through a haze of exhaustion: the final landing at the top of a stairwell, old cardboard boxes spread out on the ground, a warm radiator he could lean his back against, remaining silent, motionless, claiming nothing, conscious only that, on the whole earth, this was his only refuge, the ultimate goal of his endless trek.

That day he was skirting a forest of fir trees that still retained its wintry air – imprisoned and weighed down by the snow. At one bend in the road a woman appeared in front of him, walking in the same direction and drawing a sledge behind her. He quickened his step, glad to find himself in an inhabited area. The woman did not turn at the crunching of ice beneath his boots. He was getting ready to speak to her but suddenly recognized what load the sledge was bearing. A little coffin whose rough, unplaned planks full of knots were neither wrapped in Turkey-red cotton, as was the custom, nor even painted. The wood reminded him of ammunition crates.

They greeted one another in silence and walked along side by side. The cemetery, covered in snow, looked like a forest glade. The grave, evidently dug that morning, was not very deep and already dusted with snowflakes. The spadefuls of frozen earth thrown in by the woman resounded noisily against the wood of the coffin. When it was all over, Alexeï leaned forward to place the last clods of earth on the little mound. As he stood up again the trees, the figure of the woman and the crosses all pitched forward in a rapid curve, flying up towards the wan void of the sky. He did not feel as if he was falling.

Consciousness returned to him amid a smooth, fluid motion. He saw the crenellated fringe of the forest, processing slowly past him on his right, then, slightly raising his head, observed, at first uncomprehendingly, these two legs, these huge soldier's boots, sliding along the frozen road. He grasped that it was himself, this inanimate body, being pulled forward by the woman on her sledge. Sometimes the boots slithered along on the back of the heel, sometimes on their sides. Through half-closed eyelids he watched this rather bumpy haulage and felt as if nothing belonged to him, neither the frozen shadow that was this body, nor what his own eyes saw, nor what was visible of him. There was nothing left of him. At the foot of an uphill slope the woman paused to catch her breath. They looked at one another for a long time, motionless, silent, understanding everything.

Her days were spent half a dozen miles distant from the village on the steeply sloping bank of a river. Here, until night fell, a human ant-heap would swarm over the site where a bridge was being built. There was virtually no one there but women. They worked with no lunch-break, floundering about in the mixture of mud and ice, and covering the snow with their bloody spittle. The first military trains must at all costs cross the bridge before the end of March. It was, they were told, an order from Stalin himself.

She brought home bread, dried fish but, above all, 'the gifts of the forest', as she explained with a smile:

pine kernels, young fir shoots, which she boiled up with semolina. To his surprise he felt himself growing increasingly separate from the wind, the earth, the cold, into which he had almost merged. But more surprising still was this simple bliss: the warm line where the woman's body touched his own at night. Just this line, a gentle, living frontier, more substantial than any other truth in the world.

One night he woke up, saw he was alone, heard the breathlessness of a coughing fit subsiding behind the kitchen door. The woman often took refuge there to conceal her sickness. He lay there, his eyes open, with an intense awareness of the life returning to him, the pleasure of breathing, the sharpness of vision recovered. The moon, delicately outlined in the blackness, proclaimed a remarkable night, hanging upon the fragile first warmth of spring. He scarcely recognized himself in this moment of return. He was someone else. 'A man,' he thought, 'lying beside a window in an unknown house, in a village he could never find again on a map, a man who has seen so many people die, who has killed many, who almost died himself and now observes this slender crescent moon in a milder sky.'

Outside the door the coughing started again and was stifled in a scrap of cloth. He thought about her suffering, this woman who had taken him in, her exhaustion, her illness. Realized it was the first time he had given a thought to these things and that this was a sign he himself was cured. He reflected that there must be a word for it, some key to understanding this suffering and this moon, and his own life, changed beyond recognition, and, above all, the simplicity with which two human beings could give one another not love, no, but this peace, this respite, this release, derived simply from the warmth of a hand.

The next day he walked to the bridge construction site. The morning was vibrant with sunlight, with streams released by the snow. Though still weak, he had the joyful sensation of thrusting down against the earth at each step.

The building work would soon be finished. The women were preparing the access track. From the mass of them there arose a hubbub of raucous voices, coughing, oaths. He went away for fear of being seen by the woman who had cured him. Or rather of seeing her amid this jostling of padded jackets covered in earth, amid these faces gaunt with hunger. Between two posts, at the entrance to the bridge, he read this slogan: 'Everything for the front! Everything for victory!'

The train that carried him back to the war a week later passed over this bridge. The same human swarm still covered the riverbank under squalls of wet snow. Alexeï reflected that plunging back to face the bullets again would now have a personal meaning for him. Not the meaning of a feat of arms, such as he had earlier striven for. But quite simply, an end to the war, which for these women would also bring an end to their wading about in the mud, amid the coarseness of those voices, amid despair.

He also recalled the words he had chanced to overhear when some officers were talking: 'You know, after the victory there's going to be an amnesty, that's for sure. They'll let out the people they locked up before the war . . .' In the thick of the battles of this last year of war he often caught himself repeating these words inside his head, forbidding himself to think of his parents and thinking of nothing else, as if in an unconscious prayer: 'Before the war . . .'

This prayer was probably running through his mind during a halt one day when he saw some young soldiers who, for want of anything better to do, were amusing themselves by hunting a squirrel. The panic-stricken beast was leaping about in the middle of a cluster of tall aspens and the soldiers, wild with glee, were shaking the trunks, driving it from one tree to the next. The squirrel finally toppled down, killed not by its fall, but by the violent recoil of a branch. The soldiers picked it up, amused themselves by grabbing its tail, whirling it around and letting go.

'Before the war . . .' Alexeï picked up the little animal, felt a slight warmth beneath the fur spilling across his palm. The soldiers went down to the river, thirsty after their sport. He suddenly sensed within himself the presence of another being, an astonishingly sensitive presence beneath the armour of indifference and toughness he had forged for himself, day after day, in battle. 'Before the war . . .'

A shout from an officer caught him unawares, still in that forgotten life. 'Here, Maltsev, do you know how to drive?'

Ever adrift somewhere far away, Alexeï replied 'Yes . . . I used to have a licence . . .' If he had not had the warm body of the squirrel in his hand, he would have said 'no' with a wariness that had become second nature. The man whose name he bore, this Sergeï Maltsev, had arrived at the front from a remote village and had little chance of being a motorist. But, still absent-minded, he was replying in his old voice: '. . . before the war . . .'

Thus it was that he took the place of a general's wounded driver, one General Gavrilov, who had previously been only a name to him.

A squirrel. An ill-considered reply given to an officer. A new assignment that probably saved his life during those months of the last battles. The laughter of the young soldiers as they hunted the creature down: most of them had been killed since then. The march past of European cities – some in ruins, some in their pristine state. Some skies crowded with bombers – other skies clear, with the provocative heedlessness of clouds, birds, sun . . . He often thought about these things, aware that the disorderly torrent of life and death, of beauty and horror, ought to have some hidden meaning, a key that might give a rhythm to it all, shaping it into some kind of shining, tragic harmony.

But everything continued to happen by accident, like the explosion that hurled their car off the road one day, deafening him and obliging him to carry the badly-bruised general, trudging for long hours through a wet forest streaked with little streams of icy water. When the general came to, and learned that Alexeï, himself hit by a shell splinter, had carried him over long miles, he pronounced in solemn tones and with tear-stained cheeks: 'My dear Maltsev, from now on you must think of yourself as a son to me.' Alexeï listened to him, embarrassed by this effusiveness, his attention caught by only one detail: the name of a city he had noticed on a signpost, as he crossed a road, bowed under the general's weight. Salzburg . . . And there on this road, despite the weariness and pain, he had been aware of a distant echo, distorted by the throbbing of the blood in his temples and the general's groans. 'Before the war . . .'

Even more difficult to decipher amid this spate of accidents, be they happy or painful, was the end of the war. For neither he nor the general had noticed it. The division under Gavrilov's command was fighting in Austria, where the war continued for a good two weeks after victory had been celebrated in Berlin. The general's car ploughed up and down roads cratered by shells, everywhere soldiers could be seen vigorously engaging in hand-to-hand combat, the HQ rang with hoarse voices bellowing orders into quivering handsets.

And then one afternoon there was silence, the victory long since past, and the genial triteness of a young lieutenant's words when he accosted Alexeï, his hand on the car-door handle. 'Hey, Maltsev, I've just spent two days trying to find you! Stone the crows, we don't half look grand in our big motor! I suppose we don't recognize old friends any more . . .' As he carried on joking. Alexeï was trying to guess at the past, unknown to him, that lay behind these scraps of mockery. This friend, an old schoolfellow. The life in their native village . . . 'Your folk didn't know what to think. Everyone thought you were dead or missing. Why didn't you write, you swine? Now look. Once we're demobbed we're going home and we'll celebrate. Right? And don't you worry about that scar: it'll make the girls love you all the more!'

He had the illusion of an instant transit from Vienna to Moscow, as if the streets of the two cities ran into one another, with no frontiers. His meeting with the lieutenant, his apprehension about the life that lay in wait for him, about the life stolen from a dead man, had telescoped the weeks of repatriation together, muddled up the two cities, catapulted his car straight from the Graben onto Arbat.

And when, one day, after depositing the general at his home, he parked the car on one of the boulevards and plunged in beneath their greenery on foot, this Moscow seemed a good deal more unreal to him than the foreign cities he had passed through.

In the courtyard a child was zigzagging on his bicycle around a sandpit, the wheels squeaking shrilly, just as they had before. For a moment Alexeï thought that the child himself had not changed, that it was still the same boy who, in a past that had become quite improbable, had stared up at a young man hidden behind a dusty window. On a bench a chess player was bent over his moves. The same one? A different one? At the other end of the bench sat a man, still young, with one leg. He was reading a humorous magazine and from time to time he burst out laughing. It was clear that he was already accustomed to his condition and had made a study of comfortable positions for his disabled body. At each guffaw the chess player gave a start, settled down again, peered uncomprehendingly at the soldier's laughing face.

Alexeï pulled his cap down over his forehead and climbed the stairs. A crowd of young girls burst out onto one landing, rushed downstairs in a twittering cascade. He realized that the passage of time provided a better mask than the peak of his cap.

On the wall, beside the door of their flat, he saw three bell-pushes, three rectangles of paper with names on them. A communal flat . . . Back in the courtyard he located two windows on the façade: the kitchen, his parents' bedroom. Washing hung there, in abundance and great variety. The irresistible way life had of taking root like this seemed to him at once touching and futile.

During those first weeks in Moscow he often heard talk of amnestied prisoners who did not have the right to enter the big cities, but could settle in the Urals, Siberia, Central Asia. He pictured his parents in one of these remote places, and told himself that in time, by embarking on circumspect research, he might be able to find them again. And that from now on only his false identity risked jeopardizing such a reunion.

The general was promoted even further and now worked at the Ministry of Defence. He had doubtless forgotten his promise to treat his driver like a son but still remained benevolent and one October day when they arrived at his home, even said to him: 'Look, you come up with me. I've got paperwork to sort out, it'll take ages . . . Yes, yes. I'm not going to have you freezing out here in the car in weather like this . . .'

They went up. A silent, elderly housekeeper showed

Alexeï into a little room beside the entrance hall and brought him a glass of tea. The room, half cloakroom, half lumber-room, had a tiny window, outside which the flakes of the first snow were floating down. He immediately felt very much at ease in this quiet corner, as if the place signalled a homecoming at last. Absent-mindedly he watched the snowflakes slipping by: it was as if they were fluttering past on a day long ago, onto a forgotten city. The tea, too, had a flavour of old times. As did the silence of this vast apartment at nightfall. As did the invisible presence of the housekeeper, whom he heard sighing in the kitchen. And suddenly, muffled by the corridor, a few hesitant notes sounded. Then a whole melodious phrase. Then this music.

He left the room, took a few steps along the corridor, had no desire to go further. What he saw was enough for him. A deep-blue velvet dress, the glow of fair hair, a right hand he could see when it slipped along towards the high notes, the left hand, whose pressure he could guess at without seeing it. He remained motionless in the dim light of the corridor, his shoulder against the wall, conscious that the universe had just attained perfection. The snow outside the window, the mystery of this huge unknown apartment, this music. Above all, the imperfection of this music! For from time to time the hands came up against a combination of notes difficult to separate out, went back a little, regained their momentum. These deviations, he sensed, were essential to the plenitude of what had just been revealed. Impossible to add anything at all to it. Except, perhaps, the glance from the old housekeeper as she walked mutely along the corridor and gave him a brief look that seemed to him both understanding and bitter. Nothing else.

But these moments, which would have been enough for him, were extended and gave rise to further times spent waiting in the little room, then to the first meeting ('Oh, so you must be . . . yes, Papa told us about you . . .') and to other meetings, and to the beauty of the open, smiling face of this girl of seventeen, to the delicacy of that hand when they first touched ('Stella . . . It was Mama who chose my name . . . I think it sounds awfully silly with my patronymic, Vassilyevna, don't you?'), to the conviction that the deep-blue tone of the velvet dress was the key ingredient, at once overt and coded, of happiness. And that the other ingredients were the snowflakes outside the windows, the early dusk, and the notes whose hesitations occasionally hinted at the youthful fragility of the fingers.

He was living out this love in the past, drawn back towards the years of the great terror, when the long-nosed masks were everywhere he turned, those three years of his youth when he should have experienced exactly what was happening today: this encounter with a girl of his own age, first love. He was twenty-seven now. But the girl at the piano made this question of age irrelevant, for he felt he was outside the ordinary current of days, in a parallel time, in which he could relive those three years spent amid the masks.

Sometimes he came to his senses, observed his life as if over the bannisters of a staircase, with a feeling of giddiness: so many living and dead people stood between him and the girl at the piano. He clenched his fists, the powerful, scarred fingers, remembered that these hands had killed, had learned to handle female flesh boldly – the flesh of that woman with yellow, feline eyes, whom he had met at a friend's birthday party, at the end of the summer, and had taken when she was half asleep, drunk, experiencing something akin to disgust at this big, indifferent, lazy body . . . Remembering this, he told himself that it would have been better if he had stayed in the car, not accepted the general's invitation . . . But in the little room where he drank his tea and which the general, a sailor in his youth, referred to as 'the crow's-nest', he forgot everything and blended into the swirling of the snow, the sound of the notes, and the anticipation of those footsteps whose rapid tread he knew, and that voice: 'What are you doing here in the dark? Come along . . .'

Stella would seat him beside her, begin to play, sometimes asking him to turn the pages of the music: 'I'll give you a signal, like this, with my chin.' He did her bidding, watched her face, pretending to look out for the signal, occasionally stole a glance at the music and rapidly turned his eyes away.

She found in him the stuff of dreams, easily moulded by her young girl's imagination. This Sergeï Maltsev was someone sufficiently well defined, the native of a little village, a man of twenty-seven (which is to say almost an old man for her at seventeen), and with his brow furrowed by that horrible scar. So, a man who, to all appearances, was not the one she was secretly waiting for.

But on the other hand, he was sufficiently enigmatic: a man who had certainly made plenty of female conquests, but who, according to Stella's father, lived alone, somewhere in the snowbound streets on the outskirts of Moscow, a silent man, who often brought the general home as night was falling and disappeared into the same night, in driving rain or swirling snow. At moments like this he could easily be pictured in the guise of a mysterious stranger, whose face and life story she was constantly reshaping. Besides, had her father not one day told her that this driver had saved his life during the war?

Little by little she was caught in her own game. She needed this man who drank his tea in the 'crow's-nest'. She needed to summon him, to see his face, to forget his face, no longer to see his soldier's uniform, to picture him as pale, refined, handsome (which he was too, in his way, but differently), to dress this shade in black, to thrust him on-stage into plots she had dreamed up the previous night.

Beyond that, all she required of this stand-in was that he listen to her practising and turn the pages of her music. One day he missed the brisk movement of her chin, their agreed signal. She stopped playing, saw him sitting up very straight on the chair beside her, his eyes tightly shut, as if seized by a bout of pain.

'Don't you feel well?' she asked him anxiously, touching his hand. He opened his eyes and murmured: 'No, no, it's all right . . .' staring intently at the fingers lightly resting on his hand. After a moment of embarrassment she exclaimed: 'I've got a brilliant idea! I'm going to teach you to play a little yourself. Oh yes, you can. It's as easy as anything. It's just a children's song . . .'

The tune was called 'The Little Tin Soldier'. Alexeï turned out to be a clumsy pupil of modest abilities. Stella often found herself obliged to tug at his stiff fingers, so as to guide them towards the right keys.

Thanks to 'The Little Tin Soldier' she was able to elaborate her scenarios. The man she had at her beck and call could be scolded, flattered, sweetly tormented, complimented on an arpeggio well played, comforted after a mistake. She was discovering one of the most intensely appealing aspects of love, that of making oneself obeyed, manipulating the other person and depriving him of his liberty with his own fervent consent.

This man's silence, as he drank his tea peacefully while waiting for the general, no longer satisfied her. Now she wanted to make him talk, make him tell her about his life, about the war, to marvel or be jealous as she listened to his tales.

One day, under insistent questioning, he tried to

venture into this wartime past but felt utterly at a loss confronting recollections in which everything led to partings, solitude, death. He guessed that what she was expecting from him was a love story set against the backdrop of war, but his memory was struggling among the bodies of mutilated men, among the bodies of women possessed in haste and vanished beyond recall. All he was left with was the smell of iodine on a woman's hands, but how could he talk about that, especially to this young girl, as she listened to him wide-eyed? Talk about himself? But who was he? That soldier washing in a pool of water, after a bout of hand-to-hand combat, while the water turned red, with his own blood and the blood of those he had just killed? Or that youth shaking a dead man to get his boot off him? Or else that other one, watching at a dusty window, in another life, in a forbidden past? No, what was most real in all those years was the day he lost consciousness in the cemetery, when he was as good as dead and when all there was between him and the world was that unsteady line: an unknown woman sleeping beside him and giving him her warmth . . .

Under the pressure of her questions, he began talking about the squirrel: a halt on the march, a fine spring day, the little animal flying from tree to tree. Suddenly he remembered how the story concluded, broke off, became confused and invented a vague happy ending. Stella gave him a sulky smile. 'Papa told me you fought like a hero ... And you tell me about a squirrel! Pooh ...'

He fell silent, remembering the smooth warmth of the fur in the palm of his hand. Everything that had happened after that, he now realized, was linked to the killing of that animal: his assignment with the general, very probably his survival, his coming to Moscow, and his meeting with this young Stella who was now engaged in teasing him. She must have guessed that this man, whom she thought she had tamed, domesticated, had unspeakable deeds, shameful actions and sorrows hidden away in his life, as in an underground cave. And the fact that his demeanour in front of her was embarrassed and tongue-tied gave him a childish air.

'I didn't mean to offend you. Not at all. It was very amusing, the squirrel ...' she said, and put her hand on his, which still held the cup of cold tea. The moment lasted. Outside the window the dusk became tinged with deep blue. The fronds of hoar-frost writhed across the windowpane. Somewhere at the end of the corridor, the general's voice could be heard growling into the telephone. She shook his hand gently, as if to rouse him: 'Now, let's practise our "Little Tin Soldier". All right?'

During those weeks of great frosts she did not herself notice at what moment her make-believe story became confused with reality. Perhaps it was the evening when she proposed that they use first names. Or later, when they chanced to meet outside the entrance to the block of flats: he had just driven the general home, she was returning from her music lesson. With a resolute step she climbed in beside him and they went for a drive along the streets of Moscow, in a slow progress through the white flurries.

Or perhaps it was that other night. Her parents, in Kiev for the birthday of an old fellow soldier of the general's, decided to stay there for one more day and asked Stella to warn the driver. Having waited in vain for them at the station, Alexeï rang the bell at the apartment and she told a lie: her father, she said, was going to telephone late that night . . . Alexeï saw that she was wearing a pale lawn dress, a summer frock, and had piled her curls high in a style that gave her a formal look. Her cheeks were burning, as if with a fever.

Heroically, she made a show of nonchalance, inviting him into the reception room, offering him dinner ('They may not telephone till one in the morning. There's no point in our dying of hunger . . .'), opening a bottle of wine. Beneath the very thin fabric of her dress her body was shaking, her movements betraying an ill-controlled brusqueness that she tried to pass off as casual bravado. Alexeï realized that everything in this improvised soirée had been so well, so feverishly well prepared, that only a walk-on part was left to him. The whole scenario could have been acted out without him, in Stella's daydreams.

But he was there and understood that at any minute now his turn would come to play the part, to speak the lines, to step into a role that was at once obvious and absurd.

He stooped to pick up first a napkin, then a piece of bread she had dropped in her excitement; he poured wine, in obedience to a theatrically imperious wave of her hand; but most of all, taking advantage of his ghostly state, he was observing this girl, who appeared almost undressed in her summer frock. Her bare arms with their bluish veins that looked as if they had been drawn on with schoolboy's ink, her neck pink with excitement, her slender waist and, when she turned towards the stove, the delicate contours of her shoulder blades. He listened to her voice as it grew increasingly resonant and elated, sensing that the moment was approaching when he would have to embrace these shoulders, feel the delicacy of the shoulder blades beneath his hands.

He did not desire her. Or rather, it was quite another desire. For this night with her he would have been ready to . . . He saw himself reliving the war years and had the feeling that he would have gone through them all again for this one evening. But what was being acted out that night was intended for someone other than himself.

She had already drunk three glasses and was eyeing him in a brazen manner, at once aggressive and vulnerable, that he found painful. 'Perhaps we should ring them now,' he suggested, glancing at the clock. 'No,' she cut in, 'it's still much too early!' Clapping her hands together, she declaimed in the tones of a circus ringmaster: 'And now, our musical programme!'

She swung round on the piano stool, seized a piece of sheet music and beckoned to him. He saw it was the Rachmaninov elegy she had worked on several times without success. She attacked it, managed to clear the first few hurdles with the courage of drunkenness, fell at the next. Started again, no longer concealing her anger, stumbled . . .

He listened to her, his eyes half closed, absent-mindedly. At the third, almost desperate attempt, as she hesitated again, he murmured, without thinking: 'There's a sharp there . . .'

She broke off, looked at him. The effort of reading the music must have cleared her mind for a moment. She saw this man, sitting motionless beside her, his eyes closed, a man she had for a moment believed capable of saying what she had heard. ('I really am drunk,' she thought.) He looked very old and exhausted, and the pink spots left by the stitches on the scar across his brow were clearly visible.

He roused himself when he heard her weeping. Her elbows on the kèyboard, she was sobbing, trying to speak: 'You can go now, Sergeï. They won't be coming till tomorrow. You have to be at the station at nine o'clock . . .' Despite her tears, a conspiratorial tone lingered in her voice. This was the admission she had rehearsed as part of the night's scenario.

And then there was that other evening, in March, when the streets, roads and buildings were blotted out by a snowstorm, the last one of the winter. And it was also the last time the general invited him up to the 'crow's-nest' to drink tea.

Stella came in to see him, they remained for a moment watching the white fury outside the window. She had shut the door when she came in and the sound of her mother's voice reached them, muffled by the interminable corridor, calling out to the housekeeper: 'Vera, give the hall floor a wipe with a cloth, will you? That driver's left snow everywhere.' Stella pulled a wry face and made a gesture, as if seeking to make up for these words, then suddenly leaned over towards Alexeï as he sat there, his cup of tea in his hands, and kissed him. He felt her lips on his brow where it was marked by the scar . . . Out in the corridor a cloth could be heard scrubbing the floor.

The following day he was due to leave with the general, who had several garrisons in the North to inspect.

The inspection trip lasted almost a month. They travelled back and forth across regions still immobilized by ice, skirted the White Sea, drove through forests where for the moment not a glimmer of spring could be sensed. Just as if winter had returned. As if the days of the war had returned with the columns of troops being reviewed by the general, the tanks with their tracks grinding the frozen earth, the bleak concrete of the defence works.

With every mile of their return journey it seemed to them as if they were taking short cuts back into spring. And the only remaining trace of those wartime winters was the sheet of ice on which the general one day slipped and sprained his ankle. Alexeï had to carry him to the car. 'Do you remember, at the front, Sergeï?' he said, with a quiet chuckle. 'You lugged me along under the Fritzes' noses for eight miles.' And, without admitting it to themselves, they both had the thought that if they could laugh about it now the war really was over and done with.

In Moscow this springtime laughter could be heard everywhere. In the April sunshine that already burned the skin just as it did in summer, in the clatter of the trams on the gleaming steel rails, in the carefree faces of the crowds of young people for whom the war was no more than a childhood memory. And it was such a pleasure to remain outdoors that it no longer even occurred to the general to invite him to come up and warm himself and drink tea.

Stella realized that the winter had been a long dream, sometimes dream, sometimes nightmare, from which she was now well and truly awakened. In the little 'crow's-nest' room Vera, the maid of all work, piled up the coats, strewed the furs with mothballs. The tiny window, bombarded by sunlight, was blocked up with a thick rectangle of cardboard. In this place now it was impossible to imagine a man sitting there with his cup of tea, a man disfigured by a white scar across his brow and wearing a soldier's uniform.

But it was still more improbable to picture him walking at her side in these springtime streets, meeting her schoolfellows. No, no! The very picture of such a couple made her distraught. Besides, how had she ever thought that one day she could reveal this man's existence to the circle of friends round which her whole life now revolved? Talk to them about that dinner with him, her stupid tears? No, it was a long winter's hallucination which the sun had dissipated.

She did not care to admit to herself that this fantasy had enriched her, that, thanks to this soldier hidden away in the 'crow's-nest', she had learned a multitude of feminine wiles, so useful for manipulating a man; that he had been her toy; that she had used him. In an attempt to silence these disturbing little admissions, on one occasion she began to play 'The Little Tin Soldier', trying to imitate the mistakes he generally made, laughing at them, almost without forcing herself. Then she played 'The Waltz of the Doves', which she had also taught him, a much more cheerful tune but one which suddenly made her sad.

She experienced the same sadness when one day she caught sight of him through the drawing-room window. The car was parked in front of the entrance, waiting for the general. Stella saw the open car door, a hand holding a cigarette and, mirrored in the windscreen, the pale shape of his face. 'He'll spend his whole life waiting,' she thought and felt guilty, for in her case too many good things lay in wait for her: this beautiful spring, then, after the exams, the end-of-term ball, then university, the intoxicating freedom students have, and then . . . All she could picture was a vast surge of brilliance in the days to come.

During these moments of compassion, she also felt gratitude towards him. Why, in the course of that stupid dinner he could have undressed her, taken her, she could have become pregnant! The idea was so appalling, so compromising for her future, that she shook her head to be rid of it. And began to loathe him, for he was, in fact, in a position to ruin everything, almost without wishing to do so.

Ultimately this whirligig of regrets, joy, pity, anger and faded dreams made the exciting newness of this spring all the more piquant. Real life was about to begin.

He saw Stella only once more during these weeks of sunshine. One evening, instead of going home, he parked the car in the street behind a news-stand. He knew it was the day for her music lesson. She came into view, wearing a light summer coat, and walked along the avenue where the trees were still barely tinged with green. Her silhouette stood out against the blue of the dusk with a clarity that hurt his eyes. For a long time after she had disappeared he retained the picture of her there, at the turning off the avenue, and in the palm of his hand felt the very real sensation of touching her, of gripping the delicate outline of her shoulders with his fingers. The sensation was familiar to him: the suppleness of the dead squirrel on his palm.

He drove off, plunging into the streets, now blue, now shafted with streams of copper from the sunset. He told himself that in this life there should be a key, a code for expressing, in concise and unambiguous terms, all the complexity of our attempts, so natural and so grievously confused, at living and loving. This beautiful evening in Moscow a year after the war's end. That pale cream coat disappearing round a corner. The unbearable pain and the futile joy contained in that moment. The memory of the squirrel and there, above the bridge, the silvery white of the clouds, just the same as last winter, seen through the window of the 'crow's-nest'.

It suddenly seemed to him as if all that had restrained him just now from getting out of the car and running after that pale cream coat in the avenue was the false name he had been dragging around with him for all those years. Violently he strove to convince himself that this was the only obstacle.

The next day he sent off a request for information concerning his parents, signed with this false name.

A week later the general told him to come up with him to his office at the Ministry. For a moment Alexeï thought Gavrilov was going to talk about Stella, that he might even say: 'You know, my daughter has told me she's in love with you . . .' This crazy hope survived for a few seconds and lingered only to show him later how blind one can be when one is in love.

'Listen, Sergeï,' the general began in embarrassed tones, 'yesterday some information about you was passed on to me . . . mere rumours, I hope. But these days, as you know very well, you can't be too careful. It appears that someone's been using your name or, at least . . . How can I put it . . . ? Well, his family claim that you've taken, that is to say, not you yourself, but . . . To cut a long story short, they think their son's still alive. They know a friend saw him just before being demobilized but that he, you that is, don't want to go back to the village and you're in hiding. No one really knows why. Phew, it's complicated. The fact is, it's a case of false identity, see what I mean? And, especially in the army, that's no joking matter. I don't have to tell you that. You get sent to a camp for far less than that . . . Well, I'm just telling you this for your information. But if you think there's any kind of problem, you'd better tell me.

Affairs like this are like mines, you know. It's best to defuse them before they blow up in your face . . .'

The telephone rang, the general picked it up, his face grew relaxed and he began dictating a long list of food, specifying quantities of sausages and smoked sturgeon, and numbers of bottles of wine. In the crackling of the receiver Alexeï recognized the voice of Stella's mother. He was waiting for the conversation to end so he could confess everything.

The general hung up, licked his lips with satisfaction. 'We're preparing a hell of a dinner for tomorrow night. And the guests are well worth it. Future parents-in-law. Oh yes, Sergeï, time flies. When I went off to the war our Stella was just a little girl. Now, lo and behold, we're going to marry her off. Her fiancé's a really splendid fellow! And his father, this is just between ourselves, mind you, has an excellent post at the Ministry of the Interior. He's the one, by the way, who tipped me the wink about that business of the false name. It's all in the family, you see . . . Otherwise they'd have carted you off without another word. Well, you can talk to me about that later. Now, about this dinner. I'm going to need you from dawn till dusk tomorrow and half the night as well. Stella's invited all her friends. Well, engagements these days aren't done the way they used to be – all settled in private. So, you'll have to take them home in groups. The metro will be closed by then. In other words, maximum state of readiness!'

They installed him in the 'crow's-nest', all piled high with winter coats. The door was left ajar and he watched the guests arriving, couples (the fiancé's parents: the sugary waft of the mother's perfume, the father's deep bass voice), a few single people, then small groups of school-friends. Some of them mistook their way, came into the cubby-hole where he was waiting, stared in perplexity at this man motionless amid the overcoats and piles of cardboard boxes, uncertain whether to greet him or not. Several times the general asked him to take the car and fetch this or that guest of note. Alexeï did his bidding, then returned to his vigil. Vera, the housekeeper, brought him a cup of tea, almost spoke to him, changed her mind, simply smiled, with a sour little twitch.

He felt no bitterness, no jealousy, merely a pain so acute, so unremitting, that no other emotion could graft itself onto its cutting edge. Distractedly, he identified the sounds coming from the reception room that gave clues to the progress of the party. To begin with there was a merry din of voices, rhythmically augmented from time to time by deep bass notes. After this the popping of first one cork, then, suddenly, another, accompanied by shouts of laughter and squeals of panic. The words of the first toast being proposed by the general. And finally the clatter of knives and forks.

Rigid with grief, he felt nothing when, half an hour later, after a chorus of pleading voices, the music rang out. He readily recognized the polonaise Stella had been practising the previous winter. He even noted that the moment for this musical interlude was very well chosen: between the first glass that made the guests receptive and the subsequent food and drink that would dull their senses. He listened and, despite his absent state, noticed two or three imperceptible hesitations in her playing that were like secret reminders addressed to him alone and that made him feel even more isolated. The sound of clapping burst forth and this applause and some shouts of 'bravo' prevented him from hearing the footsteps running down the corridor.

And now Stella's face was framed in the doorway. 'Sergeï! Quickly! Do come! This means so much to me!' Her excited whisper was redolent of intoxication but it was more the intoxication of happiness than that of wine.

Perplexed, he got up, and allowed himself to be led by the hand into the reception room.

'And now for a surprise!' announced Stella, holding out her arms towards him as if to invite acclaim for him. 'Our Sergeï will play us a little tune. I hope you'll appreciate his performance . . . and my modest talents as a music teacher. "The Little Tin Soldier"!'

The young people applauded, the parents and the older guests found the jest rather daring but went along with it all the same, and clapped a little, not wishing to seem unduly severe.

After the darkness of the 'crow's-nest' he was blinded by the light in the reception room, embarrassed by the eyes fixed on him. Searching for a way to avoid the torment and not finding one, he had time to notice several faces, a woman's necklace with large pearls, the fiancé, a tall, dark young man, seated among his classmates. In Stella's gaze, for a fraction of a second, something like a forgotten shadow flitted by. He saw that she was wearing the pale lawn summer dress.

The applause died down. He sat on the piano stool, sensing that his grief, the block of ice that had held him frozen, was breaking up, turning into shame, humiliation, anger, the stupid crimson flush that rose to his neck, the weight of his thick boots resting on the slippery nickel of the pedals.

He performed, as in the days of their lessons, with the stolid application of an automaton. They were already laughing as he played, so comic was the sight of this soldier playing a little song about a soldier. Some of the young people sang the words of the chorus, which they knew. The wine was beginning to revive the general gaiety. The applause was unanimous. 'Bravo, the teacher!' cried one guest, whom Stella favoured with a curtsey. The bass voice of the fiancé's father rang out amid the laughter: 'Well I never, General. I had no idea that in your Ministry the drivers were pianists as well.' 'A drink for the pianist,' chanted one of the young men and several voices joined in. A glass of vodka was passed from hand to hand in the direction of the piano. Stella raised her arms and shouted, so as to be heard above the noise from the table: 'And now, the star item on the programme: "The Waltz of the Doves"!'

Alexeï put down his glass, turned towards the keyboard. Little by little the shouting and talking died down but still he waited, his hands resting on his knees, sitting bolt upright, with an abstracted air. Throwing a wink at the guests, Stella whispered, like a prompter: 'Go on, then! You start by playing middle C with your right thumb . . .'

As his hands fell upon the keyboard it was still possible to believe a beautiful harmony had been formed at random, in spite of him. But a second later the music came surging out, the power of it sweeping away all doubts, voices, sounds, wiping away the fixed grins and exchanged glances, pushing back the walls, dispersing the light of the reception room out into the nocturnal immensity of the sky beyond the windows.

He did not feel as if he were playing. He was advancing through a night, breathing in its delicate transparency, made up of an infinite number of facets of ice, of leaves, of wind. He no longer felt any pain within him. No fear about what would happen. No anguish or remorse. The night through which he was advancing expressed this pain, this fear, and the irremediable shattering of the past, but this had all become music and now only existed through its beauty.

In the dim light of a winter's morning the train seems to be feeling its way into Moscow among the clusters of tracks that twist and turn beneath the snow. Berg's concluding words mingle with the heavy jolting of the wheels, the voices and footfalls of passengers in the corridor. Knocked off balance by this arrival, which we had given up hoping for, the narrative hesitates and is then polished off in a few hurried sentences: the years spent in a camp ('I didn't even benefit from the amnesty when Stalin died. I did my ten years, right through to the last day'); then his visits to Moscow (in the hope of seeing Stella again? He does not say, no longer has time to say), clandestine visits, for he had been directed to live in a small town in eastern Siberia; a further arrest in the course of one of these trips to the capital; three years served close to the Arctic Circle, where he realized that he had finally become accustomed to that snow-hell . . . It was there, under the sunless sky, that he would learn the year and place of his parents' death.

The train stops. We take our first steps as if weight-less – after days and nights of immobility our feet plant themselves in the snow with the suppleness of a dance. In the frozen air the aggressive acidity of a big city stings the nostrils. Side by side with Berg, I walk along a dim, endless railway platform. The passengers stepping down from our train pause for a moment, irresolute, like sleepwalkers. One can sense a longing in some of them to sit down on a suitcase, curl up and go to sleep again. Berg goes ahead of me, I see him slipping along through the drowsy crowd, as it shuffles towards the station. For a second he becomes a passenger like the others, a provincial landing in Moscow at six o'clock in the morning. I watch him walking along and think of him arriving like this in the capital, in the old days, secretly, eager to melt into the crowd. I remember the end of his story: how Moscow was more dangerous than the depths of the *taiga*, how Vera, the general's old housekeeper, who once used to bring him tea in the 'crow's-nest', now gave him news of Stella's life . . .

Presented differently, all these missed encounters could have added up to a fine, tragic story. But they had been recounted in a confusing fashion amid the sounds of a train arriving in a great, dark, frozen city. And that was doubtless how they had been lived through, in the disconcerting simplicity with which broken lives are lived.

We enter the immoderately lofty station hall and in the midst of this emptiness, where it seems as if nothing personal can be said, Berg confides to me, without turning his head: 'Her husband had some problems at work at the time of destalinization. He began drinking, left her . . . She died at the beginning of the sixties, from cancer. Their son was seven. I did what I could, through the intermediary of a friend. A little money each month. I stayed up in the North. A job for madmen at fifty below zero. "Twelve months of winter, the rest is summer," as they say up there. But the pay was very good. Only the child mustn't know. They still had me on file as a repeat offender . . .'

He looks at me with a smile, holds out his hand: 'Well, then, safe journey and no hard feelings.'

I shake his hand, I see him moving away. Three Stations Square is gloomy at this hour. The streetlamps slice it up into bluish sections. The big lorries shake its frozen shell with their steely roar. The people hurrying along, wearing coats of coarse grey or black, look like something out of Stalin's time, the years of war, privation, silent heroism. Berg melts into this human tide, heads towards a metro station, is lost in the dark current pouring into the entrance. He has the same stiff gait, the same stoic determination. I manage to spot him in the crowd at the top of the staircase, then he disappears. '*Homo sovieticus*', a slightly scornful voice murmurs within me. I am too sleepy to be able to silence it.

I return to the station hall. The hours of departure advertised on the board have a surrealist air after our delay, after all those time zones I have crossed since the

Far East and, above all, after the past time inscribed in me by Berg's story. But the strangest thing of all is that Berg suddenly reappears. Yes, he is there in front of me, it is not a dream.

'I went off without asking you if you had a place to stay in Moscow. I hope you're not going to wait here at the station all day . . .'

I tell him I shall not be leaving until the last train, at about midnight, and that I'm planning to go and see a museum and before that I shall go to the first showing in a cinema, to sleep. He smiles; this plan of going to sleep in the cinema (ten kopecks for a showing, an empty auditorium and a nice warm seat) must remind him of his own past as a wanderer.

'Let me give you the advice of an old Muscovite . . .' (His voice cannot conceal a secret delight.) 'You know, you're as likely to find a hotel room in Moscow as you are to get a bed for the night in the Lenin Mausoleum. But I have an old friend, a recidivist, like me . . .'

He guides me across the city, by metro, by bus, then on foot, taking short cuts through courtyards, always with a touch of cheerful brusqueness, happy to be back on familiar territory, to be showing off his knowledge of the capital. I follow him with resignation, like a child walking along half asleep.

At the hotel weariness overwhelms me. I wake up for a moment in the middle of the day, an unreal vision presents itself to my eyes: stretched out on Berg's bed is a dark suit, it looks like a man squashed flat, emptied of his substance, a tie hangs over the back of the chair, a strong smell of eau de Cologne comes from the bathroom. Not having the strength to seek an explanation for it, I go straight back to sleep.

When Berg wakes me I do not immediately recognize him. He has put on the suit that was laid out on his bed, and the tie. His hair is sleek and glossy.

'I didn't want to disturb you before, you were sleeping so soundly . . . But it's evening already. It's six o'clock.'

On the table I see two glasses in which tea is infusing, a heating element hooked onto the window latch.

'Are you going . . . to the theatre?' I say, trying not to betray my surprise at the change.

'Yes . . . in a manner of speaking. Well, to a concert. And by the way, I thought that if you were interested . . .'

We drink the lemon tea and eat bread, the same as had been wrapped in pages of sheet music – and some slices of salami. After the meal I perform my toilet. Berg lends me a tie.

We are the first to arrive. The concert hall, at the other end of Moscow, belongs to the railways' house of culture.

We remain for a long while in a cold, ill-lit entrance hall. Berg, invisible, silent on a bench in a corner, while I pace up and down past walls decorated with photos of locomotives, from the most ancient squat ones, with their funnels comically bell-shaped, to the most modern. I also glance into the auditorium. It seems too vast to me, a concert will never attract enough people to fill it, especially in this district, miles away from anywhere! Nevertheless people begin flocking in, at first hesitantly, like ourselves, then, as their number grows, producing that slight electricity of whispering, anticipation, excitement that occurs before any performance. Once seated, they spread an agreeable tension through the auditorium. 'The magic of the theatre!' I say to myself. 'Who cares about the hall, or the stage or what's going to happen on the stage. The main thing is that something's going to happen.'

Berg has chosen a seat in the very back row, where the light hardly reaches at all. Placed at the side, looking beyond the folds of the open curtains into the darkness of the wings from whence the performers generally emerge, we can see a figure, the oval of a face.

'He must have got stage fright,' murmurs Berg, his eyes fixed on this dark corner.

He sits there, a little stiffly, with an absent air, as if rejuvenated.

Just then the pianist appears, the young man whose vigilance we had sensed as he waited in the wings. The audience welcomes him with parsimoniously polite applause. I turn to Berg to offer him the folded sheet of the programme. But the man appears to be absent, his eyelids lowered, his face impassive. He is no longer there.